Quiddy
and the
MYSTERIOUS MEGA VIRUS

by Alison Leonard

Illustrated by Harriet Dell

 LONGMAN

Chapter 1

A brontosaurus and a bug

It all began with Quiddy.

Well, it began with the Queen and Leonardo da Vinci. But Quiddy is most important in the story, so she should start it off.

Quiddy lives. Quiddy sits instead of walking, but she moves like the wind. Quiddy speaks with a machine. But most of all, Quiddy thinks. She uses a voice-machine, but her thoughts go a hundred times faster than her voice. Like this:

> *Clara's asking me if I want a drink of that disgusting fizzy orange, even though she knows I hate the stuff and she's only asking me to wind me up. She knows I know she's only doing it to wind me up, so I'm going to say no. Then I'll crack up laughing and then she'll crack up laughing too...*

No thanks.

So who is Clara? Clara is Quiddy's friend. She goes everywhere with Quiddy – almost everywhere. She has a life away from Quiddy, but that doesn't come into this story. Quiddy has a life away from Clara – mostly inside her head.

Clara's important, but not so important as Quiddy. Well, everyone is important. But I'm talking about who is important to the story of the virus – the great, the dreaded, the vile, the impossible, word-eating, computer-bashing, people-infecting virus.

So how did the Queen come into it? And Leonardo da Vinci? This is how.

It was Friday the 13th. Quiddy and Clara went to school as usual. So did everyone else. But everyone was waiting for something unusual to happen. You don't get Friday the 13th for nothing. It's only stupid, superstitious people who think something appalling, terrible, devastating and outrageous will happen on Friday the 13th. Except when there's a great, dreaded, vile, impossible, word-eating, computer-bashing virus around – which there was.

The virus was called Leonardo da Vinci.

He was a painter, wasn't he? Yes, around the year 1500. But he was an inventor too. As well as drawing and painting (nearly) everybody and everything, he invented (nearly) the helicopter, the armoured tank and the submarine. So some bright spark, 500 years later, thought that "Leonardo" was a good name for an un-inventor – a destroyer, a wrecker, vandal, saboteur, a havoc-maker, confusionist, mess-and-muddle and chaos-causer; a blower-up and tearer-down of systems, not by bombs and shrapnel, but by secrecy and stealth. By virus.

This Friday the 13th, Quiddy and Clara and everyone

else who went to school as usual knew about Leonardo. Everyone checked the school computers every time they used them, in case Leonardo should be up to his tricks again. (Who was he? Nobody knew.)

And how did the Queen come into it? Well, Quiddy and Clara's teacher, Miss Coward (and she was one) had a rotten cold that day. It was a sneezing, snorting, blocked-up, run-down, brains-converted-to-slurping-mud sort of cold. The only answer for a teacher who has that sort of cold is to switch on the "magic box" – the television.

"Childred," she said, "this bordig our lessod is goig to codcerd politics id this coudtry. The Queed is goig to oped the Dew Parliamedt. Bady fabous bed add wobed will be there. You bay watch it od televisiod add thed you will write ode add a half sides of paper od 'The Queed add Goverdbedt Today'." Thed (sorry, then) she blew her nose and switched on the television.

Quiddy, Clara and the others watched the square screen as Her Majesty, in red robes with ermine trim plus her retinue of men in gold-braided uniforms processed to the doors of Parliament. Quiddy thought that the Queen, when she turned to speak, looked a little bit nervous.

Well, you'd be nervous if you'd got all those gold-braided men watching you – and all of us lot out here as well, plus everyone else in the whole country who's got a cold and whose teacher has got a cold and is watching the television because their brains aren't good enough to manage anything else.

Clara turned, looked at Quiddy and giggled. She knew what Quiddy was thinking. She usually did.

Then the Queen started to speak.

"My Lords, Ladies and Members of the House of Commons ... "

The television camera also seemed to think the Queen looked nervous, because it moved away and panned over the faces of the "bady fabous bed add wobed" who were there.

"... My Government will take steps to ensure that this country of ours will be well and truly ... Well and truly, madly, deeply, probably, uncertainly, chaotically, devilishly, wildly, boisterously and preposterously pandemoniously governed."

The camera, which had been panning over the faces of the famous, suddenly stopped. It juddered and shook. The jaws of the famous dropped. The eyebrows of the famous shot up into the hairline.

The Queen, looking even more nervous, continued.

"Never in the history of our beloved nation has there been such a time as this – so hilarious, so ridiculous, fantastical, farcical, whimsical and bombastic. My Government will endeavour to make it ever more knockabout, clownish, side-splitting and paradoxical."

Quiddy looked at Clara. Clara looked at Quiddy. They looked round the room. Everyone was looking at each other. They were trying not to look at Miss Coward, who was trying not to look at any of them.

Miss Coward rushed to the television and turned the sound down. The Queen, looking more and more and more nervous, went on mouthing words.

"Please, Miss," said Patrick Pulgrove, shooting his hand up, "what does all that mean?" Patrick Pulgrove was a brainbox, like Quiddy. He was always interrupting teachers, so as to stop anyone getting on with any work.

"It beads ... Get out your dictiodaries," answered Miss Coward. "Add, Patrick, sidce you are so eager to do everythig, go idto the book cupboard add get out the thesaurus."

"What's a thesaurus?" asked Patrick Pulgrove.

"Sister of a brodtosaurus," answered Miss Coward.

Quiddy thought:

That's funny. What's suddenly happened to make her funny? Coward's never funny. If she's starting to get funny, then this really is Friday the 13th, and something peculiar really has started to happen.

"Maybe," said Patrick Pulgrove, "the Queen's got thesaurus-itis."

Everyone – even the ones like Geoffrey Cosford and Amelia Remington-Ffoulkes who couldn't possibly know what a thesaurus was, or even a brontosaurus – laughed their socks off. Except Quiddy and Clara, who looked at each other in dismay.

That was the first sign that the virus was starting to spread: not only to computers, not only to word-processors, where you could check and control and prevent it, but to people.

"Quiddy," said Clara, as they went home for dinner, "are you feeling all right?"

"Fine," said Quiddy, through her voice-machine. Actually, she was feeling excited. Nothing so spiflicating as this (oops, watch it!) had happened in years. "You?"

"Bit wobbly inside," said Clara. "Do I sound all right?"

"Fine," said Quiddy. She understood. Clara was wondering, just like she was wondering: did the Queen actually *know* she was speaking like that? Did Miss Coward realise she'd suddenly turned funny? Might one of them have caught a virus, too, without realising?

Quiddy whizzed ahead, then slowed down for Clara to catch up. Patrick Pulgrove passed them with a wave. Then footsteps ran up behind them. Was it the twins, Matt and Mike, who lived next door? No, it was Geoffrey Cosford, puffing and blowing. He walked alongside Quiddy's wheelchair.

"Say, sisters," he said, "surely someone silly sent something super so she suddenly starts sniggering, stopping stiff sleep-making sorta stuff, starting smart snappy stories?" He grinned at them stupidly, and ran down the avenue towards his house.

"Surely someone's started Geoffrey going crazy," commented Clara.

"Yes," said Quiddy, thinking:

> *Yes, it's crazy, maybe everyone's going crazy. But as well as wondering just how crazy things are going to turn out, I'm wondering what my dad's got for dinner because my dad's always been crazy. Well, way out. His way-out-ness doesn't confine itself to Friday the 13th. Though, come to think of it, maybe this virus-catching won't confine itself to Friday the 13th either?*

Clara gave her a quizzical look and went off down the path to her front door.

Quiddy's house was three doors on. "I'm hungry," she said to herself, as her special gate-opener opened the gate. Down the path to the front door, and her special door-opener opened the front door.

"Hi, Dad!" she said through her voice-machine as she whizzed down the hall.

"Humph," said her dad. Actually, he didn't, because he wasn't much given to speaking. He mainly made grunting noises, sometimes with his mouth open and sometimes with his mouth closed. He loved Quiddy and Quiddy loved him, but you'd never think it.

"What's for dinner?" asked Quiddy. She had a row of little buttons on the top row of her machine, all ready and programmed as "Things to say when you come home from school".

"Baked beans on toast," said Dad. (Or rather, Dad

grunted, while jerking his head at the pan and the toaster.)

Quiddy whizzed round and back down the hall. Thank goodness, everything was normal. At any rate Dad hadn't caught a virus yet.

Quiddy collected Clara and they went back to school for the afternoon. There was no Miss Coward.

Clara said, "Has she gone home with her cold, or with something more sinister?"

Geoffrey Cosford was passing their desks.

"Surely something sinister," he said.

"Oh, shut up!" said Quiddy.

A strange man walked in.

"Hello," he said. "I'm called Mr White." He was, too, very nearly. His hair was ash-blond, his eyes were pale grey, and his face was completely without suntan or even a single freckle. "I am your thingy." He pronounced it with a hard "g", to rhyme with "dinghy".

"As you know," he went on, "thingies come to supervise your thingies whenever thingies have to go off sick. Miss Coward, your thingy, has unfortunately developed a thingy, and has asked me to continue this thingy to work on thingies that you began early last thingy."

Quiddy spoke. She would have put her hand up, but she couldn't. Miss Coward had told her she needn't.

"Please, sir," she said.

"Who is that?" asked Mr White. "Why do you not put

your thingy up?"

"I know what she's trying to say," said Clara. Clara had red curly hair and lots of freckles. At that moment her curly red hair was shaking with suppressed laughter. "She means, which kind of thingy do you mean?"

"The thingy!" Mr White stayed calm. It was quite obvious to him what he meant. "Thingies, I do hope I'm not going to have lots of thingy from you. You will find that I'm not the sort of thingy you can make a thingy of. I intend you to do lots of thingies – and lots of thingies are what you will do."

Quiddy nodded to Clara. Clara nodded to Quiddy. They had the answer to their question. Mr White, at any rate, didn't know that he was talking rubbish.

But Quiddy kept her eye on Geoffrey Cosford. He looked very confused, and said hardly a word. When he did speak, it was only to mutter "Shan't!" or "Stop!" or "Shuttup!" He put his tongue out if anyone teased him. He might not have known at first that he was turning peculiar, but it wouldn't be long before he did.

Within quarter of an hour, Mr White's virus came face to face with Geoffrey Cosford's virus.

"You!" shouted Mr White. "You in the third thingy on the right! Pick up your thingy immediately!"

"So sorry, sir – slightly s-s-stumped," stuttered Geoffrey. "Say something straightforward!"

"Your thingy! Pick it up, and come out here!"

Quiddy thought:

> *Something's wrong. We're going to have a riot on our hands in a minute. How long before the rest of us pick up some bug? How long before Patrick Pulgrove can't think of a word with less than ten syllables, or sweet Amelia Remington-Ffoulkes starts calling everyone a "fat pig?"*

She whizzed to the front of the class and turned round to face them.

"This is serious," she said, through her machine. "Use your heads. Meet end of school. Then we can talk."

Clara clicked.

"You heard what Mr White said. Get out your books on South America and get on with the rainforest stuff. Geoffrey, get out there and show us the page."

"Exactly," said Mr White. "And not a thingy from any of you!"

But the end of school that day was not going to be as simple as Quiddy had thought. They wouldn't all want to puzzle together over the cause of the virus, because there was going to be an alternative attraction.

The children had just settled into a studious silence when the door opened. Mrs Proctor, the Headteacher, came in and coughed. All eyes lifted from the desks and looked at her.

"I am going round every class," she said, "to tell you about a message from the Ministry of Technological Affairs. There has been some kind of breakdown of the police computerised traffic control system. The result is that when their radio messages tell traffic to avoid somewhere it all immediately goes straight there." She coughed and looked round at them all. "I have to advise you all, therefore, at all costs to go to Midland Street and Southdown Street, where chaos is occurring. I repeat, at the end of school, you are to go to these streets. Thank you."

"Er – Mrs Thingy – er – " murmured Mr White, "don't you mean that thingies are *not* to go straight to these thingies?"

"Did you hear what I have just said?" stormed Mrs Proctor. "At all costs, you are to do what I forbid! You must go to this area of town!" She stalked out and slammed the door.

There was a stunned pause before everyone began putting their books in their schoolbags. Quiddy and Clara looked at each other, laughed, then frowned, then laughed again. This was going to be interesting.

Chapter 2

Viruses proliferate and twins fall out

Quiddy and Clara didn't join the mad rush into town to see the traffic chaos at the Midland-Southdown crossroads. Nor, oddly enough, did Geoffrey Cosford and Amelia Remington-Ffoulkes.

Patrick Pulgrove rushed up to them. His blue eyes were sparkling in anticipation.

"Come on," he said. "Drivers going crazy, policemen going wild – don't you want to see the fun?"

"No," replied Quiddy.

> *I like Patrick. He's bouncy and quick. But sometimes he's wrong.*

"We're going round to Quiddy's to try and sort our brains out," said Clara. "Amelia? Geoffrey?"

"I certainly feel in a bit of a muddle," breathed Amelia.

"Something sorta says should solve something soon," Geoffrey said, blushing.

Patrick laughed.

"Well," he said, looking at Amelia and Geoffrey, "I can see a couple of brains that need sorting out." And he ran off.

"I don't see why he needs to be so rude," said Geoffrey plaintively.

"You know what Patrick's like." said Clara. "He's such a brainbox he can't resist letting us all know we're not as brainy as – "

"Listen!" interrupted Quiddy, staring at Geoffrey.

Clara and Amelia stared too.

"He – he's all right!" said Amelia, amazed at her own perceptiveness. "Geoffrey, you're not funny any more!"

"Funny peculiar, she means. Not funny ha-ha," said Clara.

"Thanks a million," said Geoffrey. "I did feel peculiar. Did I look peculiar too?"

"Sound," said Quiddy. Between them, the other three told Geoffrey about his "S" virus. He was horrified.

"I'd no idea I was doing it!" he said. "But I knew something had flipped, because everyone looked at me as though I'd caught the raging measles."

They were at Quiddy's gate. The twins came by: Matt and Mike, who were absolutely identical except for the dimple on Matt's chin. They only spoke half a sentence each, because the other one always finished it off for him.

"Quiddy," said Mike, "What d'you – " "Reckon's going on?" asked Matt.

"Don't know," said Quiddy. "Come in, all." Thinking:

> *This'll make a good gang. Geoffrey and Amelia are a bit boring, but they'll do what we tell them. And the twins are good fun. I wonder if we can get Patrick to join us?*

She used her machine to open the gate and then the front door. She shouted "Hi, Dad!" as usual. No reply. "Gone down the allotment," she told the others. "Drinks and eats all round."

Clara knew where the milk, bread, orange and lemonade were kept. She fixed everyone bread and jam. She got Quiddy's straw and gave her the bread in bite-sized lumps.

"Come on, Quid," she said. "What on earth's going on round here?"

Quiddy's head sank down in thought, while her knee was clicking the switch on her voice-machine. She thought of all the viruses that had messed up their word-processors in the last few weeks. Her mind could see vivid pictures:

The way all the letters slid like autumn leaves down the screen, to end in a messy little compost heap at the bottom. That was the first.

The way it started to write everything backwards. Like:

The wild games it played, like inserting extra syllables into important words. Which looked odd when you were typing out your poetry project:

The year's at the spring-a-ling,
The day's at the morn-a-lorn,
Morning's at seven-and-a-half,
The hillside's dew-pearl-how-deft,
The lark's on the wing-a-ling,
The snail's on the all-forlorn,
God's is His hell-i-ven,
All's right with the wally-world.

She remembered the looks on people's faces: Miss Coward's outrage when she thought the kids were doing it just to annoy her; the twins wrinkling up their noses and their foreheads in puzzlement till their faces were creased all over, not just on Matt's chin; Patrick Pulgrove thrilled to see a computer doing something almost cleverer than he could.

Her machine-voice rasped out, "How can people catch a virus from a computer? Computers don't really get viruses – they have their disks corrupted. People only catch bugs from each other, like colds!"

"My Auntie Mary gets terrible colds," said Amelia. "Every winter."

Clara raised her left eyebrow – a trick she'd been practising and was very proud of. She turned to Geoffrey.

"Did you feel anything strange while you were ess-ing about all over the place?"

"I felt a bit sort of hot," said Geoffrey.

"That's how my Auntie Mary feels," said Amelia.

Quiddy had been working away with her knee.

"But it's not only us. It's the Queen and all," she said. "Turn on the telly."

The screen flickered into life. It was "Blue Peter". The presenters were holding big plastic bowls and wielding wooden spoons. The young woman waved her wooden spoon, grinned broadly and said,

"To make your chocolate biscuit base,
Just melt your chocs and find a place
to crush the biscuits without crumbs
mix, tip and press – and out it comes."

"They're – " shouted Mike – "rhyming!" finished Matt.

"Maybe it's a joke," said Geoffrey. "Maybe they'll stop now."

But no. Today, "Blue Peter" was all in rhyme. The next item featured some politician launching a campaign: Save the Whale, by a revolutionary method of computerised tracking. The sing-song voices of the presenters rang out in Quiddy's living room,

"The whale's turning pale
at the frightful wholesale
slaughter
in the water
as 'Blue Peter's reporter ..."

Quiddy switched off.

"Can't stand it," she said. At that moment the doorbell rang. "Go and see," she told Clara.

It was Patrick Pulgrove, bursting with news of the traffic chaos in the centre of town.

"You look like a good gang," he said, looking round at them all. "Can I join?"

"Patrick," said Quiddy. "Eat? Drink? Ideas?"

Patrick took a slice of bread and butter and spread half a jar of strawberry jam on it.

"Prangs," he mumbled between bites. "Bangs, scrapes, whinges, denials, insurance companies."

"There's no need to come out in full-blown thesaurus-itis," complained Clara.

"Sundry spiteful scrapes? Surely someone saved some?" asked Geoffrey.

"He's doing it again!" squeaked Amelia.

Patrick laughed.

"Poor old Geoffrey," he said. "You never were much good with words, were you?" Geoffrey looked furiously embarrassed.

Quiddy made her machine do a loud, howling noise to show that she was angry.

"Shut up being rude," said Clara. "We've got work to do."

Quiddy's knee was working away furiously.

"Ideas ideas ideas," she said. Inside her head, she was wondering:

> *Why does Geoffrey's virus come on and off like that? Why are some people catching viruses and some people not? How does the Queen get it at the same time as the police computer and the people on "Blue Peter"? Is there traffic chaos all over the country, or just in our town?*

Patrick answered the last question quickly enough.

"It's the same everywhere," he said. "There was one solitary policeman down there. The rest have rushed all over the place."

"Maybe it's something in the food," said Matt.

"Hey," complained Mike, "I was going to say that!"

"Well, why didn't you?" retorted Matt.

"I didn't get a chance!"

"Slowcoach!"

"Shut up!" said Quiddy. She would have shouted, but her machine only had one tone of voice. "Work!" Thinking:

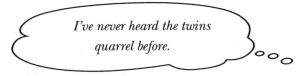

I've never heard the twins quarrel before.

"Bread, Amelia?"

"No thanks." Amelia always refused bread and jam on account of her figure. She said gently, "I can't imagine it being about food, can you? I mean, something so frightfully computerised and technological as this virus thing?"

"You've got something there," said Clara. "Patrick, haven't you got an uncle that's something high up in London? Wouldn't he know about it? Couldn't you ask him?"

Patrick stuffed another piece of jammy bread in his mouth.

"He's nothing special," he said. He swallowed. "He only goes around opening bazaars, launching campaigns, that sort of thing. No. My considered opinion is that it's influences from outer space."

That was an idea that hadn't struck the rest of them.

"UFOs?" said Quiddy.

"Could be using satellite dishes," said Patrick. "Or sending radiation through our VDU screens. Or transmitting magnetic impulses through our skin when we handle the floppy disks."

"But we use a hard disk at school," said Amelia. "It's inside the computer and we never touch it."

"That's true," said Clara. She and Quiddy glanced at each other, meaning, "Hey! One up for thick-o-Amelia!"

Quiddy thought:

Patrick will be useful. He's got computers at home. That's why he knows about floppy disks, even though we're not allowed to use them at school in case we drop them on the floor or spill coke all over them. The teachers have to do all our backing up on floppies when we've gone home.

Then she realised what the time was and jerked her head back.

"Clara!"

Clara knew what she meant:

"Look at the clock on the kitchen wall behind me. Dad'll be back soon and he'll want the house cleared of you lot." So she said, "Scram. Scarper. Skedaddle!" Then she put her hand up to her mouth. "I haven't caught thesaurus-itis as well, have I?"

"Say something simple!" instructed Geoffrey.

"Come on, you lot – haven't you got homes to go to?" said Clara, and sighed with relief.

While Dad made the meal, Quiddy worked with her knee-switch to put a full description of all the day's events into her machine, so it could churn out its excitements to Dad in a monotone as they ate their take-away pizzas. Dad made no comment, but she knew he'd taken it all in.

Then the two of them settled down with cups of cocoa to watch the news on television. The countrywide traffic chaos was the first item. 'Odd,' thought Quiddy. 'If the Queen's gone slightly crazy, you'd think they'd report that first.' Then she had second thoughts. 'No, they wouldn't. They'd hush it up and say she's suffering from flu.'

The newscaster said that all major towns had suffered havoc: they all used a computerised traffic system, logging where the traffic jams, sewage replacement schemes and burst water mains were happening that day and telling drivers where to go and where not to go. Cheltenham, Chelmsford, Birmingham, Brighton, Edinburgh, Eastbourne, Southport, Southend. Nowhere had escaped.

A grey face in a grey suit appeared on the screen, its grey eyebrows twitching. The interviewer was smarmy.

"Mr King, you are the hugely respected Minister of Technological Affairs."

'Don't overdo the flannel,' thought Quiddy.

"Multiple thanks for taking ultra-valuable time off from your hyper-extraordinary computerised whale-saving campaign."

'This isn't flannel,' thought Quiddy, 'it's downright flattery. Hey – but I've seen that man before. It's the politician from "Blue Peter"! He might be someone to watch – someone who might know the answer to the virus.'

"Have you, in your ultimate wisdom," continued the oily interviewer, "any awe-inspiring ideas as to what could have caused this apocalyptic crisis?"

Dad grunted into his cocoa with an air of puzzlement.

"I'm afraid I have no ideas," replied Mr King. "We in the Ministry of Technological Affairs are, as you might put it, totally stumped."

"So, ruinous as today's events have been, measuring sixteen point five on the Richter Scale of our national life, you personally draw a hundred and ten per cent blank on the whole cataclysmic affair?"

"Exactly," replied Mr King. "Sorry."

'Well, no,' thought Quiddy. 'He won't be much help. We might as well write him off.' But another thought was chasing round her mind, which went like this:

I think that interviewer's caught another virus.
It's not as crazy as some of the others, because we
all do it sometimes. We exaggerate. But Mr Creepy-Crawler here is
exaggerating exaggerations.
His words are going wild, crazy, over the top.

Mr Creepy-Crawler dismissed Mr King with "A million thanks for your inestimable help," and proceeded to read the next news item. "Our beloved Queen has been struck down with that most distressing of infections, influenza ..."

That night, after Dad had helped her get ready for bed, Quiddy put more notes on her machine. Every version of the virus and its symptoms, every comment from the gang, every possible cause and effect. Then, exhausted, she turned off her precious machine and lay for a while, wide awake. She didn't want to go to sleep, in case she should have dreams – nightmares – about the most cataclysmic things that could happen to her. Dreams like: that her machine caught a virus. Or that Dad or Clara caught one, so they didn't understand her any more. Or that she caught a virus herself, that ruined her special talent for understanding what people were going to say almost before they said it.

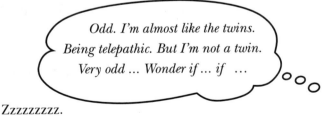

Odd. I'm almost like the twins.
Being telepathic. But I'm not a twin.
Very odd ... Wonder if ... if ...

Zzzzzzzzz.

Chapter 3

Unfunny families and an unmannerly meeting

Patrick Pulgrove didn't have as comfortable an evening as Quiddy. He ate his meal with parents, who neither spoke to him nor even looked at him. His father kept his eyes glued to the television set, his mother kept hers glued to a book.

"Strange things happened today," said Patrick, when they reached the choc chip ice-cream. (It was always choc chip. Choc chip was the only flavour his father liked.) "We had a stupid supply teacher who couldn't say any noun except 'thingy'. And the Head forgot how to say 'not' and 'don't'."

No response.

"There were six hundred and seventy-three car crashes in the centre of town."

"Go upstairs and do your homework," said his mother, without lifting her head.

"Oh – and the Queen went bonkers."

"Stop muttering," said his father. "I want to watch the news."

"Well, at any rate the news should be interesting," said Patrick to his empty ice-cream bowl. "I wonder if they'll explain what 'whimsical' and 'bombastic' mean?"

As soon as the first news item began, he said, "I told you! I told you!" But his parents' only reply was "Sssssssh!"

So he tried another tactic. He flicked the television on to a different channel.

"Hey, stop that!" shouted his mother and his father, both at the same time. But the odd thing was: his mother shouted it at his father, whereas his father shouted the very same thing at Patrick.

He went on flicking channels. Dizzy scenes of wild west lassooing, Australian soap operas and Los Angeles car chases flashed in front of their eyes.

"Stop it, please!" shrieked his mother. "If you don't quit that, my boy ..." threatened his father.

Patrick did stop. Not because he was told to, but because, as he briefly flicked on to the original channel, he had glimpsed his favourite uncle appearing on the screen.

"There's Arthur!" exclaimed his mother.

They all watched the news for a few moments.

"The man's hopeless, Irma!" exclaimed Patrick's father.

"I told you, Edgar," said his mother, "that man's about as useful as a fish in a hurricane. Switch him off." Then she turned, frowning, to her husband. "Edgar," she asked, "how was it that Patrick could change the television from channel to channel when it's you that's holding the switch?"

His father looked from the switch in his hand to his son on the other side of the table, and back again.

"What the blazes – ? Have you acquired a remote control switch of your own, boy? Show me your hands! Go on, show them!"

Patrick spread out his hands. They were empty.

His mother went back to her book, but she didn't seem to be reading it. Every so often a bewildered look passed to and fro over her face. His father got up and paced up and down in front of the fire. Patrick tried to divert their attention by telling them the amazing story of the Queen opening Parliament.

"She said that the country was going to be boisterously and pandemoniously governed!"

This was too much for his father.

"And don't tell me outright lies, either!" he shouted. He turned his back on his wife and son and switched the television on again, so that the rowdiest Texas shoot-out blotted out the horror of his own domestic scene.

His mother said, "That's enough, Patrick. Go up to your room. You're in disgrace." As he left the room, she gave him a look – not of disapproval or disbelief, but of complete incomprehension.

Up in his room, Patrick didn't feel disgraced. He found himself becoming calm and purposeful. He smiled to his image in the mirror. 'I'll show them,' he thought, not for the first time. 'I'll make them see who's boss.'

In the Cosford bungalow, Geoffrey too was having a confusing evening. Geoffrey was very close to his mother. He usually told her about everything that happened each day at school. Today, however, he was strangely uneasy and reticent.

"Come on, Geoffrey, love," said his mother, offering him his favourite pudding, apple turnover. "You're looking quite pale. What's been going on then? Someone been bullying you, have they? Might you be sickening for something?"

"It's just been one of those boring days," he managed eventually. "Boring boring boring."

"Dear dear," said his mother with a frown, pouring heaps of yellow custard over his pastry. "You're getting to be quite an adolescent."

Suddenly Geoffrey forgot his own misdeeds of the day and remembered Mr White. He could tell his mother about Mr White.

"We had this thingy, called Mr Thingy, and he gave us thingy, all about South American thingies!"

"Geoffrey!" cried his mother, shocked. "I never knew you could be so rude! Don't ever mention that word to me again!"

Angrily, she switched on the television, just at the point where the newsreader was giving the distressing information about our beloved Queen.

"Flu!" she said. "That's what it is!"

"I'm all right, Mum," protested Geoffrey, "honestly!"

"The flu! First our own dear Queen, and now my own dear Geoffrey!" She packed him off to bed after only a single bite of his apple turnover. "You'll stay there for a week and I'll bring you lots of lovely hot lemon and honey."

"A week!" wailed Geoffrey to himself, as his mother shut the door soundlessly so as not to disturb the patient.

"But I'll miss the next bit of chaos from Leonardo!"

The twins had a more ordinary end to their day. Their parents didn't watch the news. Nor did they ask their children what kind of a day they'd had at school. Matt and Mike were so telepathic with each other that the rest of the family tended to ignore them.

"What an incredible, amazing" – "mind-boggling day!" they said to each other, while the rest of the family carried on conversations of their own.

Then they paused and looked at one another with their heads on one side. They realised something – but they weren't quite sure what. Did they remember that they'd done something unprecedented round at Quiddy's – that is, quarrelled? Not quite. But they felt that something drastic had gone wrong. Now they'd recovered, they'd got their telepathy back again.

Amelia's day ended ordinarily, too. She found her mother more concerned about the stain on her schoolclothes than about the events of the day. At Quiddy's, Amelia had dropped a large blob of strawberry jam down her front. Her mother was in despair.

"It'll never come out!" she said.

For Amelia and her mother were not rich and posh, as their name and appearance gave you to assume. Mrs Remington-Ffoulkes was a larger, even sweeter version of Amelia herself, and one of Mrs R-Ff's aims in life was to present an elegant image to the world. But they were so poor that they could only afford one outfit for Amelia to go to school in. That meant a giant-sized panic if it ever got stained or torn.

Amelia didn't tell her mother anything about the mysterious word-viruses that were going round. That would only have worried her, and Mrs Remington-Ffoulkes had enough on her mind without having to get worried about that.

Quiddy dreamed that someone had invented a special computer that solved all the world's problems, like poverty and war and global pollution. Which was brilliant – except that, as it solved the first lot of problems, it created lots of different ones instead.

In the morning, after Dad had got her up and taken her downstairs, she spent the time while he was shaving and getting the breakfast in preparing for her own day. She programmed all sorts of thoughts about Leonardo into the machine. She even played back some of the previous day's events and thoughts so that she could think them over yet again.

Has it all been just a dream, like the misery-abolishing computer? No – it's real enough. The question is: what will happen today? It's Saturday. No school. Will Leonardo strike again, and if so where? And what can we – or anyone – do about it?

Clara decided that no one would want a lie-in on such a morning, and telephoned everyone straight after breakfast.

"Quiddy?" Clara's voice rang out in Quiddy's kitchen. Dad and Quiddy both grunted in response. Their telephone had a special "hands-off" mechanism, so that Quiddy could join in conversations without holding on to the receiver. "Shall we have a gang meeting? At your place?" Quiddy wasn't going to say no to that one.

Next, Clara rang Amelia. She made the mistake of mentioning the word "gang". Mrs R-Ff overheard.

"Gang, Amelia? Are you going to be climbing trees and getting your clothes torn on bushes?" Amelia managed to reassure her mother and set off to Quiddy's as soon as she could.

By the time Clara got round to phoning the twins, Patrick had already reached their house.

"Ready for a meeting?" she asked.

"You bet!" said Matt.

"I am not ready!" wailed Mike, grabbing the receiver. "Matt's stolen my best jeans and I want them back now!"

'Oh dear,' thought Clara, 'they've started that again.'

"Put Patrick on the line," she said. "I'll get him to sort you out."

In the next call, Clara spoke to Geoffrey's mother, who conveyed the sad news that Geoffrey had got the flu.

"A very severe dose," she said. "He'll be in bed for a week at least."

What Geoffrey's mother didn't know was that her son was, at that very moment, climbing out of his bedroom window. 'There's bound to be a gang meeting at Quiddy's about Leonardo,' he thought, 'and I wouldn't miss it for the world. Thank goodness we live in a bungalow!'

Clara was the first to arrive. Amelia came next. She was carrying her mother's daily newspaper – a serious paper, for as well as being elegant and anxious, Mrs Remington-Ffoulkes was extremely serious.

"What for?" asked Quiddy through her voice-machine, jerking her head towards the newspaper.

"Look at this!" said Amelia. She was quite animated. "On the front page – and all through the inside as well! She spread the paper out as best she could over the remains of Quiddy and her dad's breakfast.

Clara whistled, in a mixture of shock and laughter. Quiddy let her machine give out her howling noise – not because she was angry, but because her voice-machine couldn't say "Wow!"

I don't believe it – in this newspaper – just look! Go on, Amelia, turn over the page. (You got the message, thanks a million.) Well, what are the top people going to say about that, eh?

Peppered all over this ultra-serious newspaper were words that would get you immediately expelled if you muttered them in the corridors of school. The sort of words "Disgusted of Surbiton" complains to the television companies about when they're used in late-night films – words that people use only when they're very drunk, or very angry, or both.

"Amelia!" exclaimed Quiddy's machine and Clara together. "Has your mum seen it?"

"No," said Amelia with a little smile. "I took it from

the doormat and hid it so she wouldn't have a heart attack."

A ring on the doorbell and Patrick and the twins arrived. Then it rang again and a breathless Geoffrey appeared.

"Hey! You're supposed to have flu!" said Clara.

"You look ill," said Matt.

"No, he doesn't," said Mike, "he looks perfectly okay."

"He's all puffed!" argued Matt.

"That's because he's been running!" retorted Mike.

"Desist," said Geoffrey. "Definite decisions demand diligence. Don't distract."

Quiddy groaned inwardly. She and Clara exchanged despairing glances. It was going to be that sort of morning, was it?

They all sat round the kitchen table. Quiddy and Clara just could not control the gang meeting. Patrick seemed to be laughing most of the time. Geoffrey

spluttered D-words, mostly of five syllables like "dactylology" and "dehydrogenise", that didn't have any connection with the matter in hand. The twins quarrelled. Amelia was reduced to a confused silence.

Quiddy had been watching the clock. With relief she announced: "News." With her switch, she turned on the television.

"And now, the news," said the newsreader. Quiddy thought she looked a little pinker than usual, but it might just be a fault in the colour of the screen.

"First, the Queen. Her Majesty is not suffering from flu. She is not confined to bed. Doctors believe that it is not necessary for her to cancel engagements for at least the next five days.

"The situation as regards the police computerised traffic control system. Scotland Yard has issued a statement, declaring that the system has not broken down. Traffic chaos has not taken place in major towns and cities all over Britain. Insurance companies are not intending to put up insurance premiums on account of the sudden rise in the number of claims..."

"It's like the Head!" shouted Matt. "It's not, stupid," shouted Mike back at him. "It's just the opposite!"

"Sssssh!" said Quiddy and Clara.

"... were not summoned to an emergency debate in the House of Commons this morning. The serious state of the country will not be discussed at length, and the urgent necessity of finding both cause and cure for these problems will not be brought to Parliament's attention."

By this time, the newsreader was undeniably red in

the face. The camera mercifully shifted to scenes of angry demonstrators in the centre of some town or other.

Quiddy looked round at everyone – and everyone looked back at her. Patrick was laughing, his blue eyes crinkling at the fun. The twins were still muttering furiously at each other. Geoffrey seemed to have decided he'd better not say anything else, since the rest of the gang only got irritated if he spoke.

Amelia spoke first.

"I think the twins are both right. The newslady does seem to have caught a virus like Mrs Proctor. Only it's like an opposite one, which makes people say things aren't happening when they really are."

"No!" said Quiddy. Clara thought Amelia was right and hadn't any idea why Quiddy didn't. So they all had to wait while Quiddy used her knee-switch till she'd tapped in the whole sentence. "We can't be sure, because they might be saying that things haven't happened when they actually have, so as not to make people worried or angry."

"Denials denoting deception?" asked Geoffrey. "Doubt dawns ..."

"Stop wittering on in that stupid fashion!" said Patrick. He suddenly looked pretty furious. "Quiddy's wrong. They never tell outright lies. The woman's obviously got one of those viruses." He got up from the table. "Sorry, I've got to go now. We might be having some relations coming to stay."

When Patrick had gone, Amelia said quietly, "I wonder if things will be a bit easier with just the six of us."

"He's good fun, is Patrick," said Mike. Matt said, "But he makes me feel uncomfortable, somehow." Quiddy thought:

Something is dawning and it's not doubt. Patrick makes me feel uncomfortable, too. He's either full of fun or very angry. He's like a see-saw – you never know which way he's going to tip. He certainly makes Matt and Mike quarrelsome. Well, there's only one way to find out whether he's responsible for the really serious stuff...

She glanced at Clara. She knew Clara was thinking what she was thinking.

"What do you think, Geoffrey?" asked Clara.

"I wish he wouldn't go on all the time about how stupid I am," said Geoffrey.

His words were followed by a long silence of realisation ...

Chapter 4

A gang parliament and a Parliament perplexed

Matt and Mike turned to Quiddy. "You mean," they said together (even though Quiddy hadn't said anything) – "that if Patrick isn't here" (said Mike) – "no one" (said Matt) "gets a virus?"

Quiddy nodded.

"It seems like it," said Clara.

"I'll kill him!" cried Geoffrey.

"How beastly of him," breathed Amelia. "But what about the Queen and 'Blue Peter', and the traffic thingy?"

"You're not allowed" – said the twins – "to say thingy."

"But was he near me," asked Geoffrey, "every single time I went funny-peculiar?"

"What about that very first time," said Clara, "when we were going home for dinner, and you went on about sniggering, and smart snappy stories?"

"Did I go on like that?" said Geoffrey, amazed. "Yes – Patrick was there. I remember – he ran off in front of me just before I reached my road."

All this time Quiddy had been working up to saying something long.

"We don't know about other viruses," said her voice-machine. "Patrick can't do them – too far away. But he does it here. So what can we do?"

"Well, I don't know about the rest of you lot," said Geoffrey, "but I don't want to go on with this gang business. I'm going home. I'm going to get flu properly this time and when I go back to school I'm going to be as nice as pie to Patrick Pulgrove so he won't want to attack me ever again."

"Coward!" accused Quiddy.

"It's all very well for you," said Matt. Mike went on, "He hasn't got at you yet." "You don't know what it feels like," said Matt, "being taken over by this bug" – (Mike) "that messes up the way you talk" (Matt) – "and changes you into a different sort of person!" (both twins together).

"Matt – Mike," said Amelia hesitantly, "do you think yours really is a virus? I mean, I know you go different, but it's only quarrelling. You say normal words. Not like the Queen and Geoffrey."

"I think it really is a virus that the twins get," said Clara. "It spoils the way you talk. It breaks the threads somehow. And that's what the viruses are doing, isn't it?"

Again, a chill fell over Quiddy. She thought:

> *I need Clara. I need Dad. I need my talking machine. What if any of them went out of action? What if I was left alone and couldn't get through to anyone? I'd feel as if I was locked behind a television screen with the sound turned off, everyone out there in the room chatting merrily and not realising I'm here.*

She shivered.

"Boys are right," she said. "We don't understand. But stick together."

"Yes, we've got to stick together," agreed Clara. "We needn't let Patrick know that we've sussed him. We could just watch him and try to see how he does it."

"You could have flu for a day or two, Geoffrey," said Amelia. "Just to please your mother. Then you could come back into the gang."

"We'd help," said Quiddy. "Tell everyone not to laugh. Stop you twins quarrelling."

"How?" asked the twins.

"Er... we could stand between you and Patrick whenever he comes near you," suggested Clara.

But Quiddy let out a howl from her machine. Clara realised immediately what she meant.

"No, we couldn't. If we did, then Quiddy and I might catch a virus and wouldn't understand each other either, like the twins!"

"See!" cried the twins.

"Now you know what it's like to be scared!" said Geoffrey.

"I'm scared too," said Amelia. "I mean, what if I caught a virus that made me say all those rude words like the ones in the newspaper? What would my Mum do?" Amelia looked round for an answer, but nobody had one. "All the same," she went on, "I'd feel safer, somehow, if we stayed as a gang."

"I feel like that too," said Clara. "If some of us got a virus, the rest could tell them and help them out. What d'you think, Quid?"

There was a pause as Quiddy prepared what she wanted to say.

"Stick together," she said. "Watch Patrick. Find the cause. Find the cure."

Though, all the time her machine was speaking, she was thinking – and she suspected the others were thinking too:

> *What if we all catch a virus at the same time? Who will help us out then?*

But no one said it. There was a murmur of "Okay then," round the group. They all agreed that Geoffrey should climb back through his bedroom window before his mum found out, and stage a convincing attack of flu through the weekend. On Monday he'd bounce back to health, and they'd all go into school. Then they would discover just what Patrick, and whoever else was playing Leonardo, was going to get up to next.

Clara came round to Quiddy's on Sunday. Dad went down to the allotment, even though it was pouring with rain. The two girls sat in front of the television.

On Channel One there was a boring old black-and-white film. On Two there was "The Universe and Us." On Three there was rugby. And on Four there was "Parliament This Week".

"Would you believe it!" said Clara, switching off. "We'll have to play Monopoly!"

But Quiddy used her special switch to turn Channel Four back on.

"What on earth do you want ...?" began Clara. But she dried up into silence as they watched what was going on at the Special Emergency Session in the House of Commons.

The Speaker was standing up and waving her arms about.

"Will Members please realise," she was saying, "that the situation is serious. My duty is to keep order in this House." That was ordinary enough. But Madam Speaker went on: "And in order to fulfil that duty, I ask you all to stop shouting, sit down and listen to my jokes. What d'you get when you drop a grand piano down a coalmine? A flat miner!" The Speaker collapsed in laughter at her own joke, while all the men and women on the benches giggled like nervous children.

"They've got one," said Clara.

"Bad," said Quiddy.

A man from the Opposition Front Bench stood up.

"Madam Speaker," he began, "can Members of this House answer the most vital question of in the history of the world – that is: Where did Caesar keep his armies?" Silence. "Up his sleevies, of course!" His fellow members fell about hysterically.

Then fifty MPs stood up at the same time and started to shout different things all at once. Quiddy and Clara could just make out some of it:

"What do you get if you cross a sheep with a kangaroo?" "Why do birds fly south?" and a whole chorus of "Knock knock, who's theres."

Just then, the back door opened and they heard
Quiddy's Dad come in. Quiddy started working away on
her machine at what she wanted to say to him. He
grunted and swore as he took off his dripping wet jacket.
He must have heard the roars of laughter from the
television as he was pulling off his muddy boots because
he put a sodden, puzzled face round the door.

"Uh?"

The backbench Members of Parliament had just got
round to a series of elephant-in-custard jokes. Dad came
and stood between the girls, and stared.

"Dad," said Quiddy in her monotonous, mechanical
voice. "What happens if Government breaks down?"

"Call in the Army," said Dad gruffly and stomped off
upstairs for a bath.

Come Monday morning, the gang (minus Patrick
Pulgrove) gathered early at Quiddy's house. Clara had
summoned them, "We can wait outside Quiddy's gate

and look out for Patrick – then watch him to see what he does to start the virus."

They were all nervous. Mike and Matt kept on nudging each other and tittering; Amelia's breath was coming out in puffs and sighs; Geoffrey tapped his right foot in little rhythmic tunes until it got tired, then started with his left foot.

"Relax!" ordered Quiddy. But nobody could.

"Hi, gang!" Footsteps ran up. Patrick's blue eyes twinkled at them all. "What'll go on today, d'you think, then?"

"Nothing," said Quiddy.

"Hopefully," said Geoffrey. Was he going to start on "h" words today? He thought he'd better stick at one word at a time.

Clara tried to stare out those bright blue eyes and failed. The twins refused even to look at Patrick, never mind speak to him.

"Of all the flipping things to happen," said Amelia, as they set off towards school, "catching a flipping word virus is the flipping worst, I should flipping think. My flipping mum said this flipping morning – "

Quiddy kicked her voice-machine switch.

"Amelia!"

Amelia turned. "What do you flipping well want, Quiddy?" she inquired sweetly.

Quiddy made her machine do its frightful howl and then say, "Flipping!"

"What do you flipping mean?" asked Amelia.

"She means, why don't you flipping shut up?" said

Clara briskly.

The twins caught on and took up the refrain.

"Put a flipping sock in it" (said Matt) – "shut your flipping trap door" (said Mike) – "pipe flipping down" (said Matt) – "hang the flipping phone up!" (said Mike). Then they did a war-dance together on the pavement, because they were so glad not to have got the anti-telepathic virus today.

Amelia frowned, blushed and stuttered.

"Well, of all the flipping – "

Geoffrey took up the refrain –

"Get the flipping message, Amelia!" Then he joined the twins in their war-dance. What a relief – it was Amelia's turn today, and not his!

"Oh," said Patrick. "Today's flavour's flipping, is it? Flipping wonderful, isn't it, for a flipping minute and a half. Then it gets pretty flipping boring, don't you flipping think?"

"Flipping does," agreed Amelia, looking puzzled. They all walked on in silence, pretty flipping puzzled too.

But Quiddy, as she whizzed along in front with the wind in her hair, was thinking about Patrick, and remembering what he'd looked like during the last few days. Pictures came up in her mind, and she thought:

*We've been mesmerised by his bright blue
eyes. We haven't watched what's going on with the
rest of him: his hands, for instance. He never takes
his right hand out of his pocket. I know boys always
have their hands in their pockets – but they usually have both
hands in, or both hands out. Keep an eye on that right hand,
girl ...*

When they reached the school door, Patrick said airily,
"Oh, by the way, we might be having a visitor today."

"A visitor?" asked Clara. "What d'you know that we
don't?"

"My uncle," said Patrick. "He came to our house
yesterday. I told you, he's terribly boring. Posh public
person, all that boring stuff. He'll probably give us some
dead boring speech."

"Boring!" said Quiddy.

"Hey!" said Clara, as she swung through the doors
after Patrick. "Got a new virus, have you? Can't say
anything but 'boring'?"

This time it was Patrick who blushed, deeply – right to
the roots of his hair. His beetroot cheeks looked very odd
beneath his bright blue eyes. He turned away, overtook
Quiddy in her chair and ran off along the corridor
towards the classroom.

Quiddy turned to Amelia.

"How are you?" she asked.

"All right, thank you, Quiddy," breathed Amelia.
"Please, will you tell me truthfully – have I been saying
anything peculiar?"

"Well, yes," said Clara.

"You were saying" – "'flipping' all over the place," said the twins.

"Gracious," gasped Amelia. "I simply mustn't do it at home. What would poor Mum say?"

"You just be glad it wasn't anything worse," grunted Geoffrey. Amelia turned pale at the thought.

There was an adult cough beside them, and Mr White passed by, "Come on, children," he chivvied. "We must be quick with registration this morning. There's a Very Important Person coming to speak in assembly."

"Don't you mean," chorused the twins, "a very important thingy?" But Mr White had hurried on.

Just then, they heard the sound of a large limousine drawing up outside the main door. That was odd because all the teachers were instructed to park their cars behind the library, so as not to run down the kids coming in and out of school.

Car doors opened and closed. Everyone stopped to look. Mrs Proctor came through the doors, followed by a tall, grey-haired man in a steel-grey suit, with a steel-grey moustache to match.

Mr White, ashen-faced, shouted impatiently from in front, "Thingies!" he called. "Did you not hear the thingies I gave you? Go immediately to the thingy, hang up your thingies, then proceed with all thingy to the thingy. The Very Important Thingy has just arrived!"

Quiddy recognised the Very Important Thingy – Patrick's uncle – immediately.

Chapter 5

Arthur the King and Amelia the Unexpected

Quiddy looked at Clara. Clara looked at Quiddy. Then they both looked at Geoffrey and Amelia and the twins. They nodded to each other. They'd all seen "Blue Peter" and they all recognised this Very Important Man now being smarmed all over by Mrs Proctor. He was the man on the television who had introduced a revolutionary method of computerised whale-tracking. No one but Quiddy had seen him later, on the news, being smarmed all over as hugely respected and hyper-extraordinary by an interviewer who seemed to have caught a flattering virus. But she would tell them about that later.

They watched Mr King being ushered along the corridor by Mrs Proctor and other simpering staff. They seemed to be wafted along to the Hall as if carried by Very Important Air.

All the children of the school began to push and shove their way behind the important party. Patrick must have lost himself among them because he was nowhere to be seen.

The gang moved slowly, at the back of the crush. Quiddy had said, "Sit front!" The others knew she meant: "Go in last, after everyone else – then we can sit at the front of the Hall and watch the man carefully. No one ever wants to sit at the front, so if we go in last, we'll be able to." It was amazing what complicated concepts you could get over to people in a few words, if you were all on the same wavelength.

Mrs Proctor had just stood up and was clearing her throat when the gang moved hesitantly down the aisle.

"Come forward, you children. I wish pupils would not trickle in late! There are chairs vacant here at the front."

Where was Patrick? Quiddy couldn't see him anywhere. Certainly, he wasn't willing to go public and tell Mrs Proctor he was the nephew of the VIP. Shame: she'd been hoping he would come along with the gang and sit at the front. She wanted to watch what he did with his hands.

No one, she realised, seemed to be getting a virus at the moment. Was Patrick off-duty? And what in all this, if anything, was the role of his uncle?

Mrs Proctor began. "We are unutterably honoured this morning to have with us the Minister of Technological Affairs, a member of Her Majesty's incomparable Government, which showers us with essential beneficence, wisdom and dignified authority ..."

This is more than flattery. This is crawling, grovelling, oiliness, flannel, soft soap, wheedling, blarney. The smarmy virus!

"... Mr Arthur King. What a coincidence, to be so named! King Arthur, of legends long ago – famed for courage, chivalry and derring-do! Is King Arthur come to visit us again, I ask myself, to save our nation from pot noodles, video games and moral decay?"

Mr Arthur King (soon, no doubt, to be created "Sir Arthur" by Her Majesty herself) rose to his feet.

"Mrs Proctor – ladies and gentlemen – boys and girls. It is VG to be here this morning as a representative of MOTA. As you know, HMG is working closely with the DFE to ensure that Years One to Thirteen have an adequate, working or expert knowledge of VHS, VCRs, VDUs, EDP, DTP and so on and so forth."

Clara mouthed to Quiddy: "He's got another kind of

virus!"

Quiddy wrote silently on the screen of her talking machine:

"Maybe he talks like this all the time."

"Mrs Proctor, you have cast our minds back to KAT, as I laughingly refer to King Arthur's Time. Indeed, my esteemed parents had this very ERA – Epoch Requiring

Attention – in mind when they named me Arthur Septimus King: ASK. I do that very thing: I ask, ask and ask again. Questions upon questions. Why are people not SS – sane and sensible? Why do they allow unruly FFs to intrude on logical sequences of RAT – Rational Analytical Thought? By 'FFs' I refer, of course, to Foolish Feelings. In other words: Blushingly Unreasonable Mawkish Frippery – BUMF."

There was a scuffling noise from nearby. Quiddy glanced along the row. Mike was scribbling with a ball-point pen on a crumpled piece of paper and passing it to Matt, who was scribbling something else on it and passing it back to Mike. They were scribbling so furiously that Quiddy thought the pen would go right through the paper and stab them each in the knee.

And there's Amelia, sitting on the far side of the twins. She's looking terribly red in the face. Is something wrong with her? But I can't think about that at the moment. I want to concentrate on what Mr Arthur King is up to.

Mr Arthur King was certainly up to something.

"Let me introduce you," he was saying, "to a boy – to, let me say, a NIP. In the old days, people of a certain age like myself used to call children 'little nippers'. Now I prefer to use a different term. You have heard me described as a VIP – a Very Important Person – which indeed I am. But I consider children – some children, though not all – to be NIPs. That is, Newly Important

People. The young man to whom I am about to introduce you is a genuine example of a Newly Important Person: Patrick Pulgrove. Come up on to the stage!"

At first, there was no reaction. Silence in the Hall, as everyone waited for Patrick to emerge from his chair. Everyone craned their necks round, including all the gang (except Quiddy, who couldn't), to see what was happening.

Then there was a slight scrape of a chair from the middle of the Hall. Patrick, looking very small and extremely embarrassed, was standing up.

"Patrick Pulgrove!" exclaimed Mr King. "A NIP of the first order! Come here, lad!"

Patrick was jostled by giggling pupils as he nudged his way along the row and out into the aisle.

"Uncle Arthur ..." he murmured.

"Uncle!" roared Mr King. "Today I am not your uncle! I am the MOTA! Have you no ESP?"

Clara and Quiddy shot puzzled glances at each other. ESP: wasn't that Extra-Sensory Perception – seeing ghosts, hearing other people's thoughts, predicting the future?

"... Elementary Subservient Politeness! Only yesterday, in the offices of one of this country's most eminent newspapers, I had to upbraid the workers for their lack of this vital element in our national life! Jump to it, boy, and do what you are told!"

Patrick seemed to gain confidence as he walked

towards his non-uncle-ish uncle. By the time he got to the steps, he leapt up them two at a time on to the stage.

"Unaccustomed as I am to public speaking," he began, his blue eyes gazing over the heads of the gang to the rest of the school beyond, "I would just like to say, from the bottom of my heart and speaking from the grass roots and on behalf of the silent majority, that we all think, sir, that you're the bee's knees, the cat's whiskers and the best thing since sliced bread."

'Two viruses at once this time,' thought Quiddy. 'The old smarmy one, and a new one called "every cliché in the book".'

Mr King smiled broadly, and put a large arm round Patrick's shoulders. Quiddy noticed that his other hand, his left one, was in his jacket pocket. Odd: Patrick had his hand – the right one – in his trouser pocket. Clara nudged Quiddy on the shoulder to show that she'd noticed it as well.

"Now, Patrick," said Mr King. "Tell all your friends out there in the Hall why RAT is good and BUMF is bad."

Patrick looked adoringly up at his uncle. Then he turned back to the audience and began to make his speech.

"RAT, that is, Rational Analytical Thought," he pronounced, "is CLASS: Clear, Logical, Acceptable, Systematic, Simple. Computers can do it better than people. Computers will, eventually, do it instead of people. BUMF is SOG: that is, Sentimental Over-Indulgent Gobbledegook. BUMF will be made redundant by RAT. In this task, RAT will be assisted by computers. In due course and in the passage of time, RAT will prevail. Computers will make human beings surplus to requirements in the world of work. Leisure will be a full-time occupation. Lying on beaches in the summer will become compulsory, as will lounging on the sofa watching the television in the winter. And your toast will always land on the floor right side up."

"A small amount of exaggeration there, Patrick," beamed Arthur King. "But you get the gist."

'Gist? Oh,' thought Quiddy: 'the General Idea, Simply Told.'

"So," concluded Mr King, "we start our great experiment ..."

"What do you think of it, eh, Quid?" asked Clara, as Mrs Proctor ushered Mr King out of the Hall followed by Patrick and a shuffling line of teachers. "Strong stuff, eh?"

"Don't like it," said Quiddy, using the key she generally kept for objecting to what Dad offered her for tea.

"Many mind-blowing messages making meanings muddled," muttered Geoffrey, coming up behind them.

Quiddy groaned. Clara said, "Messy muddle is what you sound like, Geoffrey. So if I were you, I'd shut it." Geoffrey got the point and fixed his lips tight as glue. "Hi, Amelia. What d'you think of our Patrick, then?"

"Well," replied Amelia, "I don't know about you, but I

think he was *** terrible. Imagine going up there on the *** stage and shouting your *** mouth off about being *** reasonable and all that, in front of the whole *** school!"

Geoffrey's lips came unglued as his jaw dropped to his shirt collar. The twins, who had been having a loud argument before Amelia spoke, stopped and stared at her as if she had suddenly turned into Dracula's Aunt. Clara gasped so hard that she choked and started a violent coughing fit. It was lucky they were the last to leave the Hall, and that all the teachers had gone back to the staffroom with Mrs Proctor and Mr Arthur King. No one but the gang had heard what Amelia said.

"Don't say another word!" ordered Quiddy, using the key she'd specially programmed to use when Clara was getting too bossy. Thinking:

> *This really is It. The moment when one of us gets a virus that we can't manage by ourselves – that will get one of us into real trouble. Because real trouble is what Amelia's going to be in if she doesn't stop using that word, and one of the teachers hears her. Or her mum!*

At that moment, Patrick came back down the aisle towards them.

"Oh!" said Clara, between coughs. "We thought – you'd gone to the – staffroom with your uncle?"

"No – too boring," said Patrick. "Embarrassing, more

like. Uncle Arthur's not a bad bloke, but I wish he wouldn't push me up front like that. What did you make of him?" There was silence. Patrick looked round at them. "Geoffrey?" Geoffrey looked confused and glued his lips together again. "Amelia?"

Quickly, Quiddy pressed her "Howl" button and then came out with half the sentence she'd been programming. Out came her artificial voice with its strange American accent.

"Computers are okay but they can't – "

"Uncle Arthur thinks they can do everything," said Patrick.

"That's rubbish," began Amelia. "They couldn't possibly do * –"

"They can't do telepathy." Clara got in just in time.

"Telepathy?" scoffed Patrick. "Human beings can't do that either."

"They can!" retorted Matt. "Mike and me, we do it all the time!"

"No we don't!" argued Mike.

"Stupid!" Matt shouted at him. "What do we do then?"

"We say what the other one's thinking!"

"That's what tele-thingy is, daft-head!"

"'Snot!"

"'Tis!"

"'Snot!" "'Tis!" "'Snot – "

Quiddy howled again.

"Let's go," she said. Viruses or not, they'd have to show their faces in the classroom. It might as well be now.

Mr White was already launched into Computer

Studies: Databases and their Uses.

"You will not have noticed," he was saying, "that Mr Arthur King did not mention in his speech to us that computers are not particularly useful in cases of rational thought. Databases cannot help us in thinking rationally. They do not lay out data in neat, organised columns. They do not help us to locate pieces of information in convenient ways. In other words, they do not have many uses in everyday life. Any questions?" Hands shot up all over the room. "Yes? You, boy?"

"In that case, why do we have to do all this work?"

"That is not a piece of gross impertinence," said Mr White, growing paler by the moment. "If it does not happen again, I will not send you straight to Mrs Proctor."

Giggles spread round the class, then silence. Quiddy coughed to Clara, to tell her to read (quietly) what she had fed into her machine on the way back from the Hall. Clara read, "How are we going to stop Amelia from speaking?"

"Don't know," whispered Clara. "I know – I'll write her a note."

"Do not stop whispering, there at the back!" shouted Mr White. "If it does not continue, I shall not send you to the Head!"

Clara put her head down and tore a piece out of her exercise book. She wrote:

> Amelia – don't say a thing. If you so much as open your mouth, you'll be expelled.

Then she folded it up, wrote "Amelia" on the outside and passed it along the row.

One by one, the children in the row looked at it and passed it along. Mr White droned on about how databases were not this and not that. There was one person to go before Amelia got the note. It was Linda Bannock. Linda Bannock had a little snub nose and she giggled most of the time. She could never resist temptation. She held the note for a moment and giggled. Then she sneaked a look inside it, giggled fit to bust, and nudged Amelia.

"Hey!" she whispered to her. "You're going to be expelled!"

Quiddy could hear Amelia's whispered reply from right down the row.

"What do you *** mean, Linda?"

Mr White, who had been writing something on the board, swung round.

"Not whispering! Who was that, not whispering?"

"It wasn't me," said Linda Bannock. "Well, if you see what I mean." She giggled round at everyone. "I mean, what I don't mean."

Amelia stood up.

"I'm *** sorry, Mr White," she said, in her usual sweet tone of voice. "I was *** whispering, because it seems to me that the *** school is in a bit of a *** mess at the moment, and I'm *** worried about it."

Mr White said nothing. He was now the colour of newly fallen snow. He pointed to the door. Amelia, looking puzzled, walked slowly towards it and out.

Chapter 6

Parents' problems and children's challenges

Matt squeaked, "They can't expel Amelia!" Mike growled, "Course they can if she goes on like that!"

"But Amelia's a good girl!" squealed Matt.

"Call that being good, stupid?" yelled Mike. Matt picked up his heavy computer textbook and threw it at Mike. Mike cried, "Ouch!" He grabbed his sharp mathematical compasses and shoved the pointed end towards Matt. Geoffrey jumped in and managed to grab Mike's arm away, just in time.

"Boy!" shouted Mr White. "Other boy! Which boy is not which? It is not impossible to tell the difference!"

The twins stopped scuffling and, breathing heavily, waited for the next bout of Mr White's not-nonsense.

"You are not to go straight along to the Head's office!" He pointed to the door. The twins slunk off.

The classroom was now in uproar. Some were hissing, some giggling like Linda Bannock, some were shouting, "'Snot fair, 'snot fair!" Quiddy whizzed her wheelchair over to Geoffrey and pressed buttons for a pre-programmed "Thanks! Feeling better now?"

But she wasn't going to find out whether he still had his virus. Geoffrey turned to her with lips tightly sealed, looking thoroughly miserable. She whizzed back to her place beside Clara, feeling thoroughly miserable too. The

gang was breaking up. They were losing control of events. Teachers were losing control, too; so were politicians, newspapers; so was the Queen.

> *Is this what it's for? To make everything so chaotic that some Mr Big can come striding in and take charge of us all? I asked Dad: "What happens if the government breaks down?" And he said, "Call in the Army."*

She pressed a button and out came her electronic voice into the uproar: "I want to go home."

"But it's not even breaktime yet, Quid." Clara looked just as despairing as Quiddy felt. "What's going to happen now?"

The door burst open and the twins rushed back in.

"That Mr King bloke's been walking round the school" – "No he hasn't, you nerd, Procky's been dragging him round – " "Shut up, toe-rag! And all the classes are revolting – " "Rioting, crack-brain. So old Procky says – " "She shouts it out, you mean, goofball – that in honour of King Arthur's visit she's declaring – " "You don't have to spin it out, windbag; what she said was, the whole school's got the day off."

"The day off?" A faint shade of grey began to seep back into Mr White's cheeks. "In that case, children, you may not put your books away. Then you will please not proceed quietly through the doors to the school exit."

Amid cheers, the class obeyed Mr White's every word – except one – and went home.

The gang didn't break up. Outside the school gate, they gravitated towards each other and walked home together, clustered round Quiddy's whizzing chair. It was as if they felt safer if they were near her. She tried to slow down to keep level with their despondent pace. Patrick had disappeared.

"If I understood it just a little bit, I'd feel better," said Amelia.

"Don't worry," said Geoffrey. "None of the rest of us understand, either."

"Well, at any rate we got the – " "Day off," said Matt and Mike, as one.

Quiddy let out a long, electronic sigh.

"Don't any of you realise," said Clara, "what you've been sounding like?"

Amelia and the twins looked puzzled. Geoffrey said, "I didn't say a word!"

"No," said Clara. "Because you knew that if you did, it would sound ridiculous. Now – tell the twins what they were doing."

"You were quarrelling," said Geoffrey. The twins stopped and listened. "Hassling. Fighting. Calling each other toe-rag and crack-brain. Throwing things. You'd have started sticking things into each other if I hadn't stopped you."

Matt and Mike shifted uncomfortably.

"It felt peculiar – " "Hot – like when you've got flu – " "Like rushing around with your head whirling – " "And you can't remember anything afterwards."

They walked on again, in silence. Then Amelia asked, "Will you tell me the truth if I ask you something?"

"Yes," said the others.

"Did I say anything awful? Because I felt hot and peculiar as well."

There was a pause.

"Yes, you said something awful," said Geoffrey.

"Really terrible?" asked Amelia.

"Terrible," answered the twins, together.

"Like ...?"

"Well," said Clara, "if you turn up for school tomorrow I expect Mrs Proctor will tell you to go straight home again."

Amelia clutched hold of Quiddy's wheelchair.

"You mean – I'll be expelled? For ..." (she was reaching in the darkest corners of her brain for the worst possible crime) "... swearing?"

The others nodded. Quiddy turned her head towards Amelia. As they walked on, Amelia leaned against Quiddy for comfort. "What – what will Mummy say?"

In the silence, they all imagined what Amelia's mummy would say. Quiddy just hoped that enough other disasters would be happening at the same time for Mrs Remington-Ffoulkes to be distracted. Otherwise she'd have a full-scale heart attack.

There was still no sign of Patrick. Probably he'd gone

to the Head's room with his uncle and Mrs Proctor and the staff. Whether or not Mr Arthur King was still a welcome guest in the school was only one of the questions jumping round in their minds.

By common consent they went to Quiddy's. When they told her dad what had happened, he silently gave them all drinks and slices of toast. While Clara was spreading jam on her toast and helping her to eat it, Quiddy used her knee to program in some thoughts about the day.

It's got something to do with pockets. I'm certain – with what they've got in their pockets. I don't know what that could be... Another thing: I thought at first people had got lots of different viruses. But now I think it's the same virus, but it comes in lots of different kinds. People catch it in ways that suit them – or rather, that don't suit them; like the twins quarrelling, or Geoffrey seeming even stupider than he is, or Amelia coming out with those words.

When they'd finished eating, Clara went to switch the television on. But Quiddy howled. "No! Talk."

"I'm scared," said Amelia.

"So am I," said the twins. "How'd we manage if we didn't have each other?"

Quiddy and Clara caught each other's eye. It was bad enough for the twins; but how would they two manage without each other? Then Clara's eyes shifted away, and Quiddy knew that they'd both had the same thought at the same time: 'Quiddy needs Clara more than Clara needs Quiddy'. The thought hurt Quiddy. But it was true.

Quiddy decided to be practical. She pressed the button for her first thought, about pockets.

"But what have they got in their pockets?" asked the twins.

"Some kind of machine," suggested Amelia.

"What kind of machine works from inside a pocket?" said Clara.

They put their heads down and thought.

"I know!" said Geoffrey. "A video programmer! They could be flashing numbers at us that make us work like a pre-programmed television!"

Quiddy howled again, and worked away frantically with her knee.

"Not! But like. A – " But she couldn't think of the name of what she meant. She looked searchingly at Clara.

"It's a ..."

"Remote control thingummyjig!" shouted Clara. "Yes! That's it!"

Quiddy nodded frantically. The others found themselves nodding silently in agreement. That must be it. Patrick had a remote-control device in his pocket which could squirt viruses at them whenever he came near.

"Uncle too!" added Quiddy.

"Uncle – ?" said Amelia, mystified.

"Mr Arthur King has one too!" said Geoffrey.

"That's how he could – " "make 'Blue Peter' go peculiar – " "and Parliament as well!" said the twins.

"But what about the police traffic computer?" asked Clara. "And Amelia's newspaper?"

Quiddy jiggled in her chair till she'd got the right words programmed in. They normally had a rule that no one interrupted Quiddy while she was getting ready to speak, but Amelia said tentatively, "Wasn't the traffic thing just an ordinary computer virus?"

"Yes – I think it was," agreed Geoffrey.

"Eminent newspaper," Quiddy said at last. "Said he'd been. Given lecture on national life etc."

"That's right," said Clara. "ESP and all that. Elementary Servant-like Piffle."

"That's all very well," said Geoffrey, "but where does it get us?"

"We might know how Patrick and his uncle do these awful things," said Amelia. "But what do we do to stop them, before – well, before ..."

"Before the world comes to an end?" suggested Clara.

Quiddy said, "We've got to do something!" They all agreed with her. But the question was: what?

When the others decided to go home, Quiddy said to Clara, "Stay, please." So Clara stayed.

Amelia, Geoffrey and the twins were just coming out of Quiddy's gate when they heard a shout behind them.

"Hey – gang! Have you been having a meeting?" It was Patrick.

The twins panicked. They hid behind Geoffrey and Amelia and shouted in unison.

"Run!" All four of them raced as fast as they could along the road. Patrick ran after them, shouting, "Wait! I only want to know what you're all up to!"

Geoffrey and the twins got away, but Amelia wasn't quick enough. Just as she opened her front door Patrick puffed up behind, "Amelia! Don't be mean! You won't shut me out of the gang, will you?"

Amelia, with her hand on the door handle, said in her timidest tones. "I don't think I *** like you very much, I'm afraid, Patrick." She opened the door and, turning round, added, "I'm *** sorry if you're going to be lonely, but you'll have to join another *** gang." Then she shut the door.

Unfortunately, Mrs Remington-Ffoulkes had heard Patrick shouting in the road and came towards the door to see what it was. She heard those words of Amelia's. Mother and daughter stood, face to face. Mrs R-Ff looked as though she'd just seen Satan himself come in at her front door, dressed in Amelia's school uniform.

Then her expression changed to one of extreme confusion.

"Amelia," she said faintly. "There's a dreadful buzzing in my ears and a pounding in my heart. Could you get the aspirins from the medicine cabinet and make me a cup of tea? I simply must sit down."

Amelia rushed to her mother and tried to comfort her. But the front door was wide open, and Patrick was still standing outside. Amelia's soothing phrases were peppered with the offending word.

Tears pouring down her face, Amelia banged the front door shut. Mrs R-Ff fell to the ground in a swoon. As she knelt over her, Amelia heard the distant sound of Patrick's laughter.

Meanwhile, at Geoffrey's house, Geoffrey's mother was on the telephone. The surgery receptionist thought she was hysterical and wouldn't let her talk to the doctor.

"But I must speak to him personally!" she insisted. "Last week my little boy had the flu. Now it's turned to pneumonia!"

Geoffrey, behind her, was spluttering with fury and embarrassment.

"Mum!" he said. "I didn't have flu, I haven't got pneumonia now and I don't need the doctor! It's a sort of computer virus, not a flu one. It doesn't give us all a temperature, it makes us ..."

The receptionist had gone away to consult her colleagues, so Geoffrey's mother turned for a moment to listen to what Geoffrey was saying.

"Makes you do what?"

"Say stupid sentences, shout shocking sayings. Alliterate alphabetically. Fabricate fancy fables. Produce potty paroxysms." Geoffrey was beginning to enjoy himself. "Gaily gush gossip. Twitter tongue-wagging tittle-tattle –"

"Stop!" wailed Mrs Cosford. "Doctor – is that you? Fetch an ambulance at once – my son is in a state of complete kleptomaniac collapse!"

Geoffrey said as she put the phone down.

"Kleptomaniac starts with a 'k'. And it means stealing things. I haven't got kleptomania – what I've got is verbal diarrhoea."

"Diarrhoea, as well! Oh – will this monster ever go back to being my own sweet Geoffrey again?"

Clara stayed with Quiddy. For a few moments neither of them said anything. They sat quietly by the fire while Dad pottered about in the kitchen. Each of them was thinking her own thoughts.

Clara was thinking: 'If I get a virus and can't understand Quiddy or speak for her, she'll be stuck. But even if I don't get a virus – what if I just want a holiday?'

Quiddy was thinking:

I need Clara. She needs me too, because I'm her friend and we're close and we need each other. But I need her to help me and she doesn't need me to help her. One day she'll want to go off on her own.

Maybe her parents will move house and she'll have to go with them whether she likes it or not. Or maybe she'll just find someone she likes more than she likes me. She could get fed up with always helping me. She could tell me I'm selfish for always wanting her near me. But how would I manage without her? I've got my machine – and it's brilliant – but it's so slow. Clara understands me so much quicker and ...

Clara said, "Quiddy – about you and me. How come we understand each other so well?"

Quiddy had the answer to that already programmed in.

"Telepathy."

"Okay," answered Clara. "But how does it work?"

Quiddy shook her head. "Don't know."

"Another question," said Clara. "We seem to be immune – you and me. It's as if we'd had an injection against it. How come?"

Head shake again.

"Don't know."

There was silence again, except for a shout from the kitchen. Dad had banged his elbow on the corner of the cooker.

"I'm going to try something," said Clara suddenly. "I'm going to walk straight up to Patrick and challenge him to try the worst he can do – to me."

"No!" howled Quiddy.

"Why not? If we find out how some of us can resist the virus, we can help the others to get cured."

Quiddy saw the point. She was working away with her

knee. Eventually she said, "Uncle's worse. How do we get him?" At the same time, she had another – completely different – thought.

I've always been able to do telepathy. I know what Dad's thinking – I know what Clara's thinking – I even have a sneaking suspicion what Patrick Pulgrove's thinking. There's something special about me. I want to ask Dad about it. Because there's one thing I don't know about what's in Dad's head: I don't know a single thing about my Mum.

Chapter 7

Quiddy plots and Clara succumbs

After Clara had gone home, and she and Dad had eaten their fish and chip dinner, Quiddy made a decision. She would go and visit Patrick herself – and she'd go alone.

She'd explained to Dad that they'd got the day off school on account of "some trouble". He didn't ask questions – he never did ask questions. He probably thought it was something to do with vandalism or a power cut.

"One day," said Quiddy to herself, "I'll say something so riveting that he really will sit up and take notice." Now he was sitting with half a pint of beer, reading the newspaper. Quiddy looked at the paper carefully; pin-ups, murders, banner headlines. Ah well, no viruses there.

She'd go and see Patrick. First, she must program in what she wanted to say. What did she want to say? "Patrick Pulgrove, you're a little villain and your uncle's a big villain and we'd like you both to stop it, please?" No. She'd be more subtle than that.

Dad looked up once or twice, faintly puzzled to see that Quiddy's knee was working away hard on the talking machine but she wasn't saying anything. She half-thought he might raise his bushy eyebrows at her, like he did when he was waiting for her electronic mid-Atlantic voice to come out. But no, the newspaper was more interesting than she was. Or did he simply trust her to do what she wanted without asking him first? Probably a bit of both.

When she'd finished programming, she used her knee-switch a bit more to say, "Going out."

"Oh," said Dad from the sports pages. "Clara coming, is she?"

"No."

Pause. Dad was stumped.

"Want me to come?"

"No."

A longer pause.

"I'd best get your coat on you, then."

Quiddy whizzed into the hall. When Dad had got her into her coat, she used the electronic door-opener to whizz down the path and out through the gate. As she went, a thought flitted across her mind:

I might not actually be immune to mysterious word-viruses at all. Patrick might just have chosen not to attack me until later. But I've got to take that risk.

When she got to Patrick's house, she couldn't ring the bell, so she kicked the door with her foot. She was wearing trainers so it didn't make much noise. Nothing happened, so she kicked again. There was the sound of footsteps approaching the door. Quiddy waited for it to open. She had to wait a long time because two bolts and three security locks had to be undone.

The door swung slowly open. A woman stood there. She didn't speak. She looked up at the space where a head would be if the attached body was standing upright, which bodies usually are. Then, finding nothing in that space, she moved her eyes down to Quiddy.

"I've come to see Patrick, please."

Was she amazed at the electronic voice coming out of a machine, instead of a human one coming out of Quiddy's mouth? Or had Patrick afflicted her with a dumb-making virus? Whatever it was, the woman said nothing. She simply stood aside and pressed herself against the wall. Quiddy whizzed past her down the hall.

There were several doors to choose from, and she whizzed through the one that had a light on behind it. She hoped there'd be someone in there, even though no voices could be heard – only a few electronic bleeps. Sitting in an armchair was Patrick's father, reading the *TV Times*. Opposite him sat Patrick, playing with a miniature electronic game.

Patrick leapt up.

"Quiddy! What are you doing here? I mean – how nice of you to call! Would you like a drink, or something?"

"No thank you."

Patrick's father didn't look up. His mother, who had slid silently into the room, stood and stared.

"Mother," said Patrick, "this is a schoolfriend of mine Quiddy. Quiddy – my mother, Mrs Pulgrove."

My goodness, what manners he's got – when his parents don't seem to have any! Where did he learn those from? Maybe from his uncle. Government ministers must know about that sort of thing – even if they're up to all sorts of wicked tricks at the same time.

Mrs Pulgrove gave Quiddy one more stare, then went into the kitchen.

"Patrick," said Quiddy. "I want to talk." She indicated Mr Pulgrove, still sitting in his chair.

"Oh, don't worry about him," said Patrick. "Neither of my parents ever listen to anything anyone says."

Quiddy's heart was thumping. She pressed some keys on her machine.

"Patrick, I know what you're up to. So we needn't discuss that. What I don't understand is – why?"

"Up to?" said Patrick. His blue eyes held Quiddy's. "You mean all these word viruses? I'm as perplexed about them as you are! Oh – are you wondering how I've managed to escape catching one? You and Clara have escaped, too. Maybe you two are behind it all!"

I knew he'd say that. And I'm ready for it. Ready in a way that he couldn't possibly expect...

"I'm so glad you're not responsible, Patrick." Her mid-Atlantic accent sounded somehow sweeter than before, she thought. "I was worried it might be you and I wanted to test you. But now I'm sure you're innocent. Perhaps we can plot together to catch the person who really is doing the damage?"

Patrick's yes glistened more brightly.

"Well – yes, I suppose we could. What sort of plot do you mean?"

Patrick's father turned the page of his *TV Times*. Was he listening to every word they said? Quiddy couldn't tell.

"I was thinking about your uncle," she said "He's so clever – and so important. Do you think he could help us to find the villain?"

"Oh! I'm not sure!" Patrick was so surprised that he flopped down into his mother's armchair.

Quiddy pressed the button for the next part of her speech. "Is he still at school? Could he come and see you, so we could ask him to help us?"

"Well, as it happens," said Patrick, "he's coming any minute. He said he'd have a dutiful cup of coffee with old Hatchet-face Proctor, and then he'll come along here. Actually – " Patrick leaned forward and spoke in a confiding tone – "he can't stand my parents – and they can't stand him." Surely Patrick's father couldn't be listening to *this*? "Mother says he was always jealous of her when they were children, because she was so much cleverer than him." Now it was Quiddy's turn to be surprised. "Oh yes," Patrick went on. "She doesn't say much, but she remembers everything. She says Uncle Arthur's hopeless unless he's got a machine to help him. But I think he's brilliant."

Quiddy was getting ready to ask a question. "Why is he coming here then?"

"He's not coming to see *them*," Patrick answered

proudly. "He's coming to see *me.*"

'Ah,' thought Quiddy, 'the ultimate revenge of the green-eyed brother: you come along and steal your sister's child!'

"Okay, then, Quiddy," said Patrick. "How can Uncle Arthur help us?"

Quiddy was about to tell him when the doorbell rang. Patrick said excitedly. "That'll be him now!"

But it wasn't Uncle Arthur. It was Clara.

"Clara!" said Patrick. "How nice to see you. Quiddy's here. She and I are plotting how to catch the villain."

Quiddy's heart sank.

What's Clara going to say? I haven't got time to program an explanation into my machine. Even if I had, she wouldn't be able to read it without Patrick seeing it too!

She came up behind Patrick and tried to put some expression on her face that would help. It wasn't easy. Then she waited for Clara to say something to Patrick, or to her.

Clara opened her mouth. Her lips made shapes, but no sound came out. She looked alarmed, closed her mouth, opened it and tried again. Movement, but no sound. The thing that Quiddy most dreaded had happened. Clara was struck dumb.

Before either of the other two could react, a car drew up outside. No ordinary car; it was a limousine, the one

76

that had brought Mr Arthur King to the school earlier
that day. Quiddy remembered what Patrick had said:
"Uncle Arthur's hopeless unless he's got a machine to
help him." A machine like a limo, to make him feel big.

Uncle Arthur got out and strode up to the front door.

"Well, Patrick my boy! The NIP has got some little

friends to play, eh? And one of them – " he peered
through the door at Quiddy "is a teeny bit wobbly on
her pins, is she? Bit of a spastic, eh?"

Quiddy wanted to run him over with her wheelchair
and squash him flat, there and then. She heard Patrick,
behind her, mutter "Uncle!" But she had more
important things on her mind: Clara and her plot. She
whizzed back into the living-room. The others followed
her. When they got there, Clara came and stood behind

her chair. Quiddy could hear her breathing unsteadily.

"This is Clara and this is Quiddy," said Patrick to his uncle.

Mr Arthur King nodded at Clara.

"Good morning, little Clara." Quiddy couldn't see whether Clara had opened her mouth or not. She said nothing. ('Well, I wouldn't if I were her,' thought Quiddy.) "Hello, little – er – Quiddy," he said, leaning over Quiddy's chair. Quiddy didn't press her "Good morning" key. "Well! Shy today, are we? You should take your example from our Newly Important Person here. He doesn't allow himself to be shy, do you Patrick?"

Patrick looked embarrassed. "Look, Uncle," he said, "You'll be interested in Quiddy's machine. She can't talk in the ordinary way, but she can say whatever she wants by using this switch here."

'Don't you dare mess with my machine!' thought Quiddy. As Mr King leaned over her, she jerked her knee – not to show him how brilliantly she could talk, but to give out her horrible howl.

Mr King jumped backwards. Quiddy wanted to do it again and again; to make that horrible noise until the Minister of Technological Affairs screamed out loud.

> *I want to howl, and howl, and howl. Clara can't speak – maybe she'll never speak to me again – I'll be lost without her – what on earth am I going to do?*

But she forced herself to concentrate on her plot. She found the right button on her machine to carry on with her original speech.

"We need to outwit the villains who are causing this chaos. This will require Rational Analytical Thought. That is what you are good at. Please help us."

She felt Clara's hand on her shoulder as she looked at Patrick and his uncle and waited for their reply. She could see that they were really taken aback.

"Er – " said Patrick. "We – we could help them, couldn't we, Uncle Arthur? I mean, they're worried by it all. Aren't you, Clara?"

Clara said nothing. Her breathing now sounded like panting.

"Now, kiddies," said Mr King.('Has he got a virus that makes him so contemptuous,' wondered Quiddy, 'or does it come naturally?') "Young Patrick here has given me the benefit of a blow-by-blow account of all the unaccountable happenings in the English Language department."

Clara, behind Quiddy, gasped. Quiddy realised she was longing to say something.

She wants to say, "Nothing's unaccountable in the 'English Language department', you ridiculous, pompous nincompoop. The problem is: we're either talking nonsense or we can't talk at all!"

"Now," said Mr King in the same patronising tone, "there is absolutely no necessity for anxiety. As I was detailing in my lecture this morning: when machines take over the world, there will be no need for human beings to talk to each other at all. All rational communication will take place by electronic means. Every other type of discourse will be rendered entirely superfluous."

While he was wittering on, Quiddy was preparing her next line of attack. As soon as he paused for thought, she pressed the right key. "We think they do it with some kind of remote control device. Do you agree?"

Again, she managed to cause Patrick's uncle's jaw to fall several centimetres. Straightaway she pressed the same key as she'd pressed earlier. "We need to outwit the villains who are causing this chaos. This will require Rational Analytical Thought. That is what you are good at. Please help us."

Patrick turned to Mr King. "She's right, Uncle Arthur. It's awful, what's happening to them. You should have heard poor Amelia. She's the sweetest girl, normally. But she's started to ... Well, I can't tell you what she's started to do. And Geoffrey – and Mrs Proctor – and you should just hear that Mr White ... They're terribly unhappy about it. We must help them."

Clara's hand tightened on Quiddy's shoulder. She must be realising what Quiddy's plot was. And it was working – at any rate where Patrick was concerned. She was beginning to get him on her side. Unless he was pretending ... ?

Suddenly Quiddy couldn't bear to be in Mr Arthur King's presence a moment longer. Not only that: she had to be alone with Clara, to see if this dumbness virus would go away when she was out of sight of these two villains – and out of reach of whatever they had in their pockets.

"Sorry," she said, in her usual clipped style. "Must go," and she whizzed round and out of the door. Clara had to run to catch up with her.

Clara banged Patrick's front door behind them and raced along after Quiddy. She opened her mouth to yell, "Hey, wait for me!" – but nothing came out.

She stopped, and looked behind her. No Patrick. No VIP Arthur King. No one to squirt at her with a remote-control device. Clara had caught the virus and this time the virus had stuck.

Chapter 8

Clara flips her lid and Patrick is transmogrified

Clara and Quiddy stood face to face with each other in Quiddy's back room. (Well, Clara stood, Quiddy sat.) Clara was furious. She was more furious with Quiddy than she was with her own dumbness. She glared at Quiddy, flung her arms around, stamped her foot, waved her arm violently first at Quiddy and then towards the front door. She frowned, jumped up and down, jerked her head in rage first to the left (in the direction of her own house) and then to the right (in the direction of Patrick's).

Quiddy knew exactly what she was trying to say. It was: "How on earth could you be so bird-brainedly stupid as to go to Patrick's house and risk facing not only him but his power-mad uncle as well? And to go on your own – without me! Why didn't you come to my house and collect me? How *could* you?"

Quiddy was furious too: that Clara had thought it was okay for her, Clara, to go and face Patrick, but not okay for Quiddy to go. She was so furious that, however hard she worked with her knee, her words came out in incoherent bursts.

"Why you not me – something by myself – always with you – scared – but got to – alone."

Clara went on heatedly waving her arms about and jumping up and down. As well as being furious, Quiddy was puzzled. Why had Clara come back to her house and found out from Dad where she'd gone? But that was too complicated to ask. Then she thought:

> *Did she come back to tell me she was on her way to Patrick's, and was she extra-super-furious that I went and did it instead – all by myself?*

She calmed down a little and got busy, working on something more coherent to say next.

"Fed up always going places with you. Sometimes want to be on my own. Do things on my own. Take risks. Get scared. Can't you see?" Then she pressed the key to let it come out of the machine.

Watching Clara listening to her, Quiddy saw that she was right. Clara's face changed. The fury drained away, and there seeped in its place something like dejection. First Clara stared at her; then she looked away; then she turned her back on her.

Quiddy wanted to comfort her – but at the same time she didn't want to say sorry for being independent. She decided to concentrate on the dumb virus.

"Don't worry. You'll get voice back. Find cure."

Clara turned round again. She didn't nod or shake her head. She came over to Quiddy's machine and pressed three pre-programmed keys.

"Don't know. Don't understand. Want to go home." Then she walked miserably back down the hall and out through the front door.

Quiddy sat alone. She and Dad had eaten dinner without speaking, as usual. Now Dad was out in his shed, potting plants for his allotment. There was silence. But Quiddy felt as if her thoughts were shouting in her head.

> *I wanted to do something alone. But what happened? I upset my best friend. I wanted to get Patrick to abandon his beastly uncle and help us to cure the computer virus. But what happened? Either Patrick or his uncle decided to make the virus far, far worse. So where do I go from here?*

One thing was certain, though; she had to tell the gang what had happened. She could use the phone without anyone else's help. When she had pre-programmed what she wanted to say, all she had to do was press the keys marked "Phone" and "Hands Free", then press the numbers (which she could always remember perfectly, even if she'd only used them once before).

Amelia answered the phone. When she heard Quiddy's voice saying "Come for a meeting", she replied, "Yes, of course, straight away. I'll have to leave a note for my poor mum, because she's upstairs in bed ill."

Geoffrey, oddly enough, said exactly the same thing. He'd finally managed to persuade his mum that he hadn't got diarrhoea, but then she decided that she'd got it instead.

The twins were the only ones who didn't sound as unhappy as Quiddy felt.

When the five of them had gathered in the back room, Quiddy didn't wait to explain why Clara wasn't there. She told them exactly what had happened round at Patrick's. Then they understood.

"Poor, poor Clara!" breathed Amelia. "She must feel absolutely terrible! I know I would. I'm not sure if my mum's going to speak to me ever again."

"Nor mine," said Geoffrey.

The twins were fairly sympathetic, but not so much as the others. "It wouldn't be so bad for us," said Mike. "Because we understand each other without even opening our mouths," said Matt.

Quiddy went mad. She worked away infuriatedly with her knee. "Don't you see? We won't all go dumb. Virus works differently – makes people specially worse."

"What d'you mean, Quiddy?" Geoffrey looked mystified.

"I wish you could – " "say things like everyone else" – "so we could fathom – " "what you're trying to say," said Matt and Mike.

They were so *thick!* Would they ever understand?

It was Amelia who saw what Quiddy was getting at.

"Oh! Do you mean that I specially don't want to swear, so it makes me swear – and Geoffrey doesn't want to be stupid, so it makes him stupid – and the twins want to be exactly the same, so it makes them different – and Clara ... Why has it made Clara dumb, then?"

They all waited for Quiddy's answer.

"She wants to be my voice. So she loses her voice."

"D'you think you'll ever get a virus, Quiddy?" asked

Amelia, quietly.

"Don't know," Quiddy replied. And she didn't.

"Well, I think we should get Patrick round here," said Geoffrey. "So we can see whether Quiddy's really got him on our side instead of his putrid uncle's."

Amelia turned pale at this. The twins shouted, "No! What if he gave us all our viruses again – " "and we're stuck with them for ever?"

"If you twins have got two brains between you – and not only one," said Geoffrey, "then you can come up with a better suggestion."

'Well said,' thought Quiddy. 'So long as you keep free of viruses, Geoffrey, you're really not so stupid after all.'

"It is scary," said Amelia, even more quietly. "But I think we should do what Geoffrey says. Patrick's the only one who knows how the beastly things work, so he's the one who could tell us the cure."

"But what if?" said Matt. "Just imagine," said Mike, "all of us stupid or dumb or quarrelling or swearing for ever and ever." "And the worst of it is," added Matt, "we don't realise we're doing it, so we can't understand why everyone's getting so amazed."

They looked round, and realised that the other three were gazing at them, hoping for a suggestion that was less scary than Geoffrey's. But they'd got none.

"Okay," said Quiddy. "Ring Patrick." She programmed in what she wanted to say. Then the others watched, impressed, while she operated the phone. They'd never seen her do it before.

While the phone was ringing, Geoffrey whispered to Amelia, "What happens if his parents or his uncle answer?"

But Quiddy had thought of that.

The patronising voice of Mr Arthur King boomed out of the phone.

"Pulgrove residence. Arthur King speaking. Can I help you at all?"

"Patrick to come to Quiddy's house immediately, please," said Quiddy. Then straightaway she switched off the phone so that Mr King couldn't answer back.

There was a pause.

"D'you think he'll come?" asked Mike. "He might and he might not," said Matt.

Dad came in, his hands all covered with soil. When he saw the gang, he said, "Huh!" and went into the kitchen.

"Is he cross with us?" murmured Amelia.

"Always like that," replied Quiddy.

Then they settled down to wait for Patrick either to come, or not.

At Patrick's house, Mr Arthur King went into the kitchen to see his sister. He found Mrs Pulgrove sitting on a stool reading a very long book. Patrick followed him to see what would happen.

"Stella," he said. "I've had a very hard day. Please could you make me a cup of tea?"

"There's the kettle. Tea bags are in the top cupboard. Milk's in the fridge."

"Stella! I may be your little brother, but I am also the Minister of Technological Affairs!"

"And I'm reading *War and Peace*," replied Mrs Pulgrove, without taking her head out of the vast volume. "If you want a cup of tea you can make it yourself."

Uncle Arthur turned round to Patrick. "That's the trouble with this country of ours," he said. "No one shows respect for authority. Take your friends, young man. That little crippled thing in the wheelchair. She tried to challenge me in my own department! 'Rational Analytical Thought', she said. As if children could be capable of such a thing! As if cripples could come and tell Government Ministers how to run the country!"

Something changed inside Patrick. He suddenly had doubts about his uncle. Perhaps it was the word "cripple" that did it. A switch inside Patrick flicked off – the switch marked "Uncle Adoration" – and a switch marked "Uncle Suspicion" flicked on.

In the same instant, a flash of inspiration struck – like lightning. Only it wasn't lightning, it was Power. He, Patrick, could have power over Uncle Arthur! If Uncle Arthur had given him the ability, through his remote control device, to inflict viruses on everyone else, then he could use that same device to infect Uncle Arthur!

He felt in his pocket. The instrument lay there: tiny, neat, super-charged. He stroked it gently.

"I know what I'll do," he said to himself. "There's that old story that says, 'If you make a daft or an ugly face, and then the wind changes, you'll be stuck with it forever.' Well ... I'm not the wind, and it may not be Uncle Arthur's face. But something drastic is going to change ..."

Uncle Arthur was saying, yet again, "I am Minister of Technological Affairs!"

Patrick pressed his powerful device.

"Are you wanting a cup of tea, Uncle Arthur?" inquired Patrick.

Uncle Arthur nodded vigorously. "I am the Minister of Technological Affairs!" he replied.

"Do you take milk and sugar?"

Uncle Arthur shook his head vigorously. "I am the Minister of Technological Affairs!"

"And how about a biscuit?"

"I am the Minister of Technological Affairs!"

"Oh dear," said Patrick's mother, her head still deep in *War and Peace*. "Arthur seems to have got his words stuck in a groove. It's just like when he was a little boy. He always said the same thing over and over again – only then it was 'It's not fair'!"

Uncle Arthur shook his fists and raged like a little boy. "I am the Minister of Technological Affairs! I am the Minister of – "

"Yes," said Patrick as he filled the kettle for their tea. "So you keep saying."

Words had failed Mr Arthur King. He set upon Patrick like a tiger upon a deer.

The gang of five sat glumly in Quiddy's kitchen as they waited for Patrick. Quiddy's dad joined them. Twenty minutes passed. Twenty-five. Thirty.

"I think we should – " "go home," said the twins.

"Um ... I mustn't be too long, either," said Amelia.

"I'm really not sure ... " said Geoffrey. At that moment, the doorbell rang.

Quiddy whizzed along the hall and opened the front door. The others held their breath. One thought was in all their minds: 'What horrors might Patrick bring with him?' – with another thought rushing up behind: 'What if his putrid uncle comes too?'

It was Patrick, on his own. His jacket was rumpled and torn. His hair was standing up like twigs in a high wind. His face was glistening with wiped-away tears. He looked shattered, limp, bemused. His right eye looked as if it would blow up any moment into an enormous black-and-white bruise.

They'd all expected that, if he came, they would stand or sit as far away from him as possible. But he looked so terrible that they crowded round him.

"Patrick! What happened? Did some kids jump out at you on the way? Sit down. Quiddy's Dad can get you a drink. Tell us all about it."

Only Quiddy was cautious. Patrick might just be trying to get their sympathy.

*Okay, I can usually tell what people are thinking.
But I'm not sure with Patrick. He's got so many
layers, he's like an onion. I don't know which layer
we're seeing at the moment. I feel sort of sorry for
him – but I'm going to wait and see.*

She whizzed into the kitchen and said to Dad, "Drink
please. Biscuits too." Then she whizzed back.

"...wouldn't make him a cup of tea, and I... did
something. Then Uncle Arthur beat me up," Patrick was
saying.

"Just because she wouldn't make his tea!"

"Are you bleeding anywhere?"

"Borrow my hanky ..."

Again, while the others were sympathising, Quiddy
was thinking – and programming. Then she asked, "Just
what sort of 'something' did you do?"

There was silence.

"Come on, Patrick – tell," said Geoffrey. Amelia
nodded.

"Spill it," said Mike.

"Lay it on the line," agreed Matt.

"Get down to brass tacks," said Mike.

"Gospel," added Matt.

"I – er ..." Patrick glanced at Quiddy. She knew what
he was thinking. He was hearing his own voice, less than
an hour ago, saying innocently to her: 'You mean all
those word viruses? I'm as perplexed about them as you
are!' "I – um," he said, "thought I'd give Uncle Arthur a
taste of his own medicine. So I squirted him with a

virus."

The gang said nothing. They just stared at him, right into his bright blue eyes.

"Yes, I can do it," said Patrick, "I'm sorry, in a way. But it was fun, wasn't it? Old Coward and that White bloke and Procky Proctor and all?"

"Fun?" gasped Amelia.

"Fun!" shouted Geoffrey.

"Fun!" screamed the twins. They rushed at him, all ready to beat him up.

Patrick's arms shot up to his face. Quiddy pressed her howler and her "No!" key. The gang drew back. He'd already been beaten up by his uncle, he didn't need any more.

Silence reigned again, except for a chorus of heavy breathing. Only Quiddy was working away with her knee.

"Patrick," her voice-machine said. "Why change? Come over to us?"

Patrick sniffed.

"I had to choose between Uncle Arthur and the viruses," he muttered, "and being friends with you, gang. I chose you."

Just then Dad came in with the drinks and biscuits.

"Here you are, you lot," he said, putting them down on the table. "You look like you need something inside you."

Okay Patrick. I'll accept that, for the moment. Heavens above! Dad's talking! Maybe he's got a virus now ...

Chapter 9

Dad tells Quiddy and Arthur tells the nation

But Dad didn't say anything else. He sat down with a large mug of steaming tea and started to listen to them as the anger broke.

"You made me stupid!" Geoffrey accused Patrick. "If you're not around I'm not stupid at all!"

"You made me ..." Amelia was breathless with the attempt to say what she meant without saying Those Words, "the nastiest person I could ever imagine!"

"Rat!" cried Matt. "Pig!" (Mike) "Toad!" (Matt) "Death watch beetle!" (Mike) "You made us quarrel!" (both).

"Clara," said Quiddy. "What about Clara?"

Patrick had been looking thoroughly cowed and humiliated, but now he started to defend himself.

"It wasn't me that made her dumb! Don't blame me for everything! That must have been Uncle Arthur!"

"Other viruses only short," Quiddy went on. "Went away when you not there. Not this. Clara still dumb."

"It's awful," said Amelia. "What if she can never speak again?"

"You're going to have to do something!" said Geoffrey.

"Make your uncle –" "make her better!" said the twins.

"Yes," said Quiddy, and then did her howl. It expressed exactly what she felt, so she howled again.

"I don't know if I can," Patrick replied, miserably.

"He's bound to have got a cleverer machine than the one he gave me. Maybe his has got a switch marked 'Permanent Change' that he uses for special occasions – or for people he specially hates."

"But why should he specially hate Clara?" said Amelia.

"I don't know," replied Patrick. He drank down his drink in one gulp and said "Thanks" to Quiddy's dad in an uncertain voice. Then he said, "I feel terrible. Would anyone mind if I went back home?"

"But your uncle's there!" said Geoffrey. "Won't he beat you up again?"

"He stormed off back to London. My dad went with him," answered Patrick, brightening. "My mum was pleased. In fact, she seems quite proud of me for standing up to Uncle Arthur. Maybe now she'll talk to me a bit."

He turned to go. But Quiddy brought him back with a "Wait!" They all watched, wondering what she was going to say. "Where is it?"

"It?" Patrick's blue eyes flashed in that old, innocent look.

Quiddy looked fiercely back at him. She asked again. "Where is it?"

Patrick grinned.

"I'll tell you where it is," he said. "I threw it at Uncle Arthur. It hit him on the head and fell on the floor."

The others laughed and shouted, "Good for you, Patrick!"

Quiddy still felt a flicker of doubt – but she let it go.

When Patrick had gone off home, Geoffrey and Amelia caught each other's eye.

"Geoffrey's mum and my mum aren't feeling too good today," said Amelia. "Maybe we'd better go home too and see how they are."

The twins were just about to follow them, when Quiddy stopped them with a howl.

"Wait!" She programmed something silently on to her screen, and showed it to Dad.

"Write note to Clara," it said. Then it told him what to write: "Twins will take."

Dad did as she asked and handed the twins the scribbled note. It said, in great big capital letters:

I DON'T CARE IF YOU CAN SPEAK OR
NOT. YOU ARE MY FRIEND.

The twins had gone. Quiddy and her dad were alone. Dad went back to the paper and started doing the crossword. Quiddy thought:

Okay, I'll leave him there for the moment while I program in what I want to say. Then I'll let him have it, loud and clear. And there'll be no going back.

The clock ticked. To Quiddy, as she worked with her knee, it sounded deafening. Even the scrape of Dad's pen on the paper made her wince. Was he thinking about her? Did he wonder what she was writing? Did he ever wonder what she was thinking? He looked after her. He loved her, she knew that. But did he ever pause to ask himself what was going on inside her head? Did he, after he'd got her clean, dressed and fed and off to school, ponder what sort of individual this daughter of his might be?

"Dad," said her artificial voice.

"Mm?" Except that it didn't have a question mark at the end.

"Dad."

"Mmmmm?" Bit more of a question mark this time.

Howl. "Dad!"

He didn't look up.

"Want something?"

"You."

"Huh?" His bushy eyebrows shifted slightly.

"To talk to me."

Now he stared at her.

"Huh!"

"I want to know things. Do you want to find out what I want to know?"

"'Course." His head fell down again towards his crossword.

Quiddy pressed some more keys.

"No you don't 'cos if you did you would pay attention to me." Howl.

Dad put down his newspaper and stood up.

"Look, Quiddy. If it's something you want, I'll give it you. I don't go in for fancy talk." It was the longest speech she could ever remember coming from him. He started to make for the kitchen door.

Quiddy took a deep breath and pressed another key.

"I want to know about my mum."

Dad stopped in his tracks, with his back turned to her. Then he took another step, into the kitchen doorway.

"I've got dishes to wash."

Quiddy howled. She pressed again and again.

"I want to know about my mum. I want to know about my mum."

He stopped and turned round. His face was white. He stood like a picture in a frame: a picture called "Shock".

"Quid," he said, "there's no need for you to know."

She pressed again. This time she kept her finger down on the key and didn't let it go.

"I want to know about my mum. I want to know about my mum. I want to know about my mum. I want to know about my – "

"If you don't stop that row I'll take the wretched machine away and chuck it on the dump!"

Quiddy pressed one of the automatic keys on her machine.

"Please. Please, Dad. Please."

Dad came back and slumped down into his chair. He started to pick the soil out of his fingernails.

"All right. If you must." He sighed a deep sigh. "She left us, Quiddy love. There's no more to be said." He'd never called her "love" before.

"What colour was her hair? What colour were her eyes? Was she tall or small? Was she fat or thin? Was she happy or sad? Was she clever or dim? Did she like telly or reading? Did she grow up in town or country? Did she have brother or sister?" It all came tumbling out. Finally:

"What was her name?"

Dad put his head down into his hands.

"Listen," he said. She could just about hear. "She had your colour hair and eyes like ... someone else. She was kind of tall and kind of thin. She was happy once and sad after. She was clever at knowing things but dim at doing things. What came next? Telly and reading, both. Village. No brothers no sisters. So she wanted lots and lots of children of her own."

Quiddy was thinking:

And she only got me. I can't take it all in. It's too much. But I did ask. I don't want him to go on and I don't want him to stop. And who's this "somebody else"?

Dad paused, took a few shallow breaths and started again. His voice sounded quite different from how it did normally. It was lighter. It sounded almost frightened.

"She liked to wear pink and purple. She used lavender soap. She rode a rattly, old bike. She had her hair permed once but the curl went all frizzy and she let it grow out. She wanted a cat but I wouldn't let her. She sang 'White Christmas' while she made a pot of tea even if it was flaming June."

Hello, Mum. When I smell lavender I'll think of you. When I hear "White Christmas". When I hear a rattly old bike. When I see a frizzy perm, Hello Mum.

"She left us, Quiddy."

"Yes but why?"

"Because."

"Yes but why?"

"Because." Dad lifted his head at this point and looked at Quiddy. He must have seen suddenly that she wouldn't stop, that she wouldn't let go. He said, "Quiddy." He came over and stood beside her. He put his hand over hers. "You were twins, Quiddy. I mean, you and your sister. You had a sister."

"And?"

"And she was ... I mean to say, she wasn't going to be in a wheelchair like you."

Quiddy didn't know if she wanted to hear any more. But, feeling the warmth of Dad's hand still over hers, she pressed that key once more.

"And?"

"She got ill and died, Quiddy, your sister – when she was still a baby. And your mum didn't know what to do with herself. So she left. She said to me, 'You and Quiddy'll be all right. Thing is, she read her sister's mind. I know she did. She'll read other people's as well, I know she will. So she'll manage all right'."

It took Quiddy a little while to program in the next bit, because her knee was shaking. When she'd done it, she let Dad see it, silently, on her screen.

> *AND I AM ALL RIGHT.*

She and Dad didn't speak any more. He patted her hand and went out into the garden.

A little while later, there was a ring at the door and Quiddy went to open it. It was Clara. She grinned and Quiddy grinned back. Clearly, Clara had got her note, but obviously she still couldn't speak. Quiddy took her to the living-room, and programmed in the words: "Use my machine." Clara put up her hands in a gesture of uselessness – how could she?

Quiddy showed her what she did with her knee and her keys. Soon Clara was kneeling beside her and working away like mad. She jumped around in triumph when she managed to get a sentence written on to the screen. In no time they were having a quick and silent conversation.

Clara wanted to know everything that had happened since she'd pressed those three pre-programmed keys: "Don't know. Don't understand. Want to go home" and walked away. She was amazed that Patrick had fought with his uncle. She hugged Quiddy for her skill in getting him off Uncle Arthur's side and on to theirs.

"Now we must fight the uncle," she wrote. "But how?"

"Don't know," said Quiddy. "He's big. Powerful. Technical. In government. Us small. Weak. Not computer-good. Only children."

Clara read what she'd written, stood up and made a large gesture. It was absolutely clear that she meant: "So what?" They laughed and laughed. It was great to be communicating again.

Then Quiddy switched on the television. As it flickered into life, Clara gawped at her in surprise and mouthed, "What for?"

Quiddy had remembered something that Patrick said: "Uncle Arthur stormed off back to London. My dad went with him." Before she could explain, the scenes on television did it for her.

The programme called "Parliament Today" had never seen anything like it before. The commentator could be heard stuttering in the background: "It is by no means certain that some semblance of order will return within the foreseeable future ..." His voice was overridden by a shout across the studio by the producer: "Nigel – stop messing about! Cut! Substitute 'Neighbours' without delay!"

But before "Nigel" could grab the tape and tranquillise everyone with the familiar Australian theme song, there was just time for Quiddy and Clara and the audience throughout the country to glimpse what was happening in Parliament.

Mr Arthur King, Minister of Technological Affairs, assisted by a gentleman unknown except to Quiddy and Clara who recognised him as Patrick's father, was standing up on the seat of the Speaker's chair in the House of Commons. He was sporting (Quiddy noticed) an uncommonly large bump on his forehead. The whole assembly of members of Parliament were kneeling down and pointing at Patrick's Uncle Arthur, reciting in chorus:

"This Country Needs You! Arthur, our King, save us! This Country Needs You! Arthur, our King, save us!"

Then the kneeling MPs were replaced on the screen by tanned figures racing over sun-drenched beaches. Quiddy switched off.

That's it. He's got what he wanted. He's going to run the country, and no one will be able to stop him. Because he'll be able to make everyone say exactly what he wants them to say – and nothing else.

Clara reached out for Quiddy's hand. Her eyes said it all: "Isn't it terrible? What are we going to do?"

Quiddy's head sank into her shoulders as she worked hard with her knee. "He can hurt our voices," she wrote, "but he can't hurt our thoughts. Let's get the others round here again – and THINK!"

Chapter 10

The gang's – and Her Majesty's – plans

They all came, even Patrick. He was a few minutes later than the rest, because he was just finishing a conversation with his mother.

> *Huh! That's a sort of revolution in the Pulgrove household. A bit like the revolution there's been in mine. Dad even smiled a tiny smile and patted me on the shoulder before he went out to dig the potato patch!*

The gang sat in silence, looking round at each other. At first the others glanced furtively at Patrick, but he just stared back as if to say, "I'm the same as you now. No brilliance, no special skills. A member of the gang." As if to prove they could trust him, he searched in both his pockets for a large white handkerchief, let the pockets hang out of his trousers empty and blew his nose.

"Got to go to London," said Quiddy suddenly.

The others gawped at her.

"Why?"

She gave them a news bulletin about what she'd seen on television.

"That's terrible!" said Amelia huskily.

"This country will be a tyranny!" said Matt.

"Dictatorship!" (Mike) "We'll all be too scared to do anything" – "or say anything" – "in case it's not" – " what Mr Arthur King approves of !"

"Let's look and see if there's any more news," suggested Geoffrey.

Quiddy switched on and flicked through the channels till she found one with a news programme. The face of the neat, respectable newscaster was flushed red and she was reciting the news as if she felt the barrel of a gun against her back.

"... funding crisis in our hospitals has unfortunately brought about an increase in negative patient care outcome. It is necessary, in consequence, to issue regulations resulting in revenue enhancement tax-base erosion control. Now – sport. United experienced some dissatisfaction at the conclusion of their match against ..."

"Please, does anyone know what she's talking about?" asked Amelia.

Clara jumped up and down in frustration at her inability to speak, but Patrick said what she was thinking.

"She must have got a gobbledegook virus. What she's trying to say is that there's not enough money for hospitals, so more people are dying so they've got to put up taxes. Oh, and United lost."

They turned back to the television.

"... former Minister of Technological Affairs, Sir Arthur King, has been asked to take *ex officio* control of the newly appointed Supervisory Council. This body will *pro tem* have powers of *fait accompli,* given that the *Zeitgeist* no longer demands a *quorum* or a *quid pro quo.* Sir Arthur states that he intends to govern by *diktat* through the mass media. *Q.E.D."*

"Yes," said Quiddy. "We've got to go to London."

Clara, sitting beside her, pressed the keys on the machine to say, "Okay. But how?"

There was silence once more.

Quiddy glanced at the clock.

It's getting late – too late to go anywhere today. I've never been to London. Nor have the others, so far as I know. What will Dad say? Will he help? Find out train times, give us money? And the other parents – what will they say? But they must help us. We've got to go and sort out Uncle – Sir Arthur King before it's too late.

"Patrick," she said. "Where's your remote-control device? Your virus infector?"

Patrick showed them his empty pockets. Then he seemed to hesitate.

"Well?"

He stood up, turned round and showed them a long, rectangular bulge in his back pocket. He patted it.

"I hid it there in case Dad should grab it. Don't worry – I promise I'll never use it again. Shall I stamp on it and chuck the bits in the dustbin outside?" He took the fatal instrument out and made as if to throw it on the floor.

Quiddy howled. Patrick stopped, his hand poised high in the air.

"No!" said Quiddy.

"Why not?"

Amelia supplied the answer.

"I think Quiddy means," she breathed, "that we might need it when we get to London and face your Uncle

Arthur."

"Yes," agreed Geoffrey.

"Yes yes," nodded the twins. Clara and Quiddy caught
each other's eye and smiled.

They were on the 9.27 train next morning. Patrick said
his mother was so glad to be rid of Uncle Arthur that
she'd agreed to help Patrick in any way she could.
Geoffrey's and Amelia's mothers were terrified at the
thought of their little ones in the middle of the wicked
city. They were only pacified by Quiddy's dad speaking
to them on the phone in his strong reassuring voice. The
twins' parents scarcely noticed what was being said to
them; they handed over the fare and said, "Be good
then." Clara didn't say how she'd managed to
communicate with her family. Well, she did tell Quiddy –
but that doesn't come into this story.

Quiddy's dad was coming too. Quiddy had told him,
with a howl at the end of every sentence: "You're coming
to keep us safe. (!!) Not tell us what to do. (!!) If we need
advice we'll ask for it. (!!) If not, we're okay. (!!) Okay?"

Dad frowned grimly, but his eyes twinkled so Quiddy
knew he understood. He'd got a whole book full of
crosswords to occupy him on the train, so he didn't say a
word all the way. He didn't seem to listen to the gang
prattling on. They were making plans: where they'd go,
what they'd do, who they'd see and what they'd say when
they arrived. By the time the train drew into the vast,
echoing station, they all knew their every move.

London had a strangely quiet and breathless air. There was traffic in the streets, but it drove hesitantly, tentatively. People walked the pavements, but they didn't look at each other or speak. Shops were open for business, but they did their transactions without saying, "Sunny day for a change, eh?" or "Now, if you give me the 12p, I'll give you a 50 and we're straight." Though the air was bright and clear over the office blocks and department stores and hotels, some invisible atmosphere hung above them, for which Quiddy could only find the name *fear*.

It was when she'd summoned a taxi with a single wave that it dawned on them there was one problem they hadn't faced. What would they do for money?

"Don't worry," said Geoffrey breezily. "My mum was in such a panic about me being safe that she gave me enough cash for every emergency under the sun."

Quiddy sighed with relief. But, at the same time, she could see the people around them on the pavement looking at the gang with a mixture of astonishment and alarm. Their expressions were saying, "Chatting, merrily, on such a day as this? How could you?"

The taxi-driver said nothing as he helped them all in. He didn't even say they were too many, or complain about the wheelchair.

"Have they all been struck dumb?" Quiddy asked Clara silently on her machine.

"Where to?" asked the driver.

"Not quite dumb, apparently," whispered Clara.

Quiddy had carefully programmed in her reply to the taxi-driver's question.

"Buckingham Palace, please." Dad raised his eyebrows, but kept his lips tight shut. She thought, 'He trusts me.'

They were driving slowly, down the Mall, when Quiddy let out a howl that almost brought the taxi screeching to a halt.

"Clara!"

Clara squeaked, "I said something!"

"You can talk!" squealed the others, in chorus.

Quiddy asked, "How?"

Clara thought hard. "My throat hurt," she said. "It's been hurting since before I went to your house, Patrick."

"It's a virus!" shouted one twin. "A real virus!" echoed the other.

"Like my Aunty Mary gets," added Amelia, huskily. "Her colds always go to her throat. Then she complains about her tonsils. Then she loses her voice ..."

"Huh!" said Dad. Quiddy could feel him shaking with laughter beside her. She thought (and she knew Clara was thinking it too):

That's fine! Clara was the only one who seemed to catch a permanent virus. If Clara's okay, then it means everyone's okay, so long as they're out of sight of the villains. Or – if Patrick truly is a reformed character –

the villain. But how, with Arthur King in control of the whole country through his Ministry of Technological Affairs, are we going to stay uninfected by his viruses? More important, how are we going to put control back into the hands – into the mouths and voices – of ordinary people?

Geoffrey paid for the taxi at the gates of Buckingham Palace. They all climbed out. As Dad lifted her into her wheelchair, Quiddy caught a whiff of panic crossing his face. He was wondering. 'Does she really know what she's doing?'

The gang stood, with Dad hovering uncertainly behind them, and faced the tall bearskin-helmeted guards in their booths.

"Now what do you propose to do?" Dad growled.

Quiddy knew. She was going to say something, but it was Patrick who was going to do something. She wrote some words on the screen of her machine. Patrick laughed and moved a small rectangular object from his back pocket of his trousers to the right-hand one.

Quiddy pressed a key and made her speech to one of the guards.

"I wonder if you would be kind enough to allow us to see Her Majesty. As you are no doubt aware, a terrible virus has been infecting the whole country and has affected even the Queen herself. We have a plan to cure it. May we come in, please?"

The Guardsman laughed. His friend on the other side of the gate looked aghast. They turned to each other and shook their heads. Of course no one was allowed in on such a pretext. It was ridiculous even to ask. The security situation ... Her Majesty's privacy ...

Patrick pressed his device.

"Of course," said the first guard.

"Of course," repeated the other. They flung the gates open. The gang walked into the forecourt of Buckingham Palace. More guards, more uniforms. Quiddy pressed the key for her speech: "I wonder if you would be kind enough to allow us ..."

More laughter, more ridicule. Then Patrick pressed his device.

"Of course, of course."

Through the archways, through great oak doors.

"I wonder ..."

"Of course." Along carpeted corridors and – Clara and Patrick lifting the bottom of Quiddy's chair, Dad taking the handles – up marble stairways.

"Of course," nodded the guards. "Of course."

At last, they came to the Queen's personal private secretary. He was a tall man, thin as a stick, with small thin spectacles. He rustled a file of papers in his hand as he stepped anxiously towards them, muttering, "Most irregular – your authorisation? Ma'am does not receive in the morning..."

Quiddy pressed her key, "... affected even the Queen herself. We have the cure. May we come in, please?" Patrick pressed his device again.

The tall, thin man's face remained hostile. But his voice said. "Of course."

The gang held their breaths and walked slowly towards the Queen's door. The door creaked as it swung open. But Dad stepped forward. "No."

Quiddy jerked round to face him. She'd have howled if she hadn't been afraid it would upset the Queen inside the room. How dare he? Come hell or high water, they were going in!

"No," repeated Dad, "Not you lot. All the gang except Quiddy stay here. She's going to do this one on her own."

The gang stood back. Quiddy whizzed in.

They waited. And waited. And waited.

Dad tried to keep them occupied with crossword clues to guess at, but they might have been struck dumb for all he got out of them. The twins clutched each other's hands. Geoffrey and Amelia stood close and shrugged their shoulders at each other every thirty seconds. Clara stared at the great oak door as if, when it opened, it would reveal the secrets of the universe. Patrick thought frantically of all the viruses he might produce for this occasion, but couldn't imagine a single one which would help.

The personal private secretary had gone into the room with Quiddy. What would she say to the Queen? Had she prepared properly, programmed everything in? Would the Queen believe her? Even if she did, what could she do against Uncle Arthur?

The door opened. The stick-like private secretary came out.

"Ma'am and the young lady are completing their deliberations," he murmured. "Would the rest of the party care for some refreshment?"

They nodded dumbly and followed the tall thin shape, which now stooped as it sloped down the carpeted corridor. In a small ante-room lay a tray of cups, with tea, coffee, orange juice and lemonade laid out, plus chocolate biscuits (the wrapped kind).

"As you please," murmured the secretary, waving a twig-like arm, and vanished. The gang, plus Quiddy's dad, tucked in.

They had just finished when the secretary reappeared and coughed politely. They licked their lips, wiped their hands and waited for him to speak. He announced, "Ma'am and the young lady will see you now."

Hearts in their mouths, they followed Mr Stick Secretary back along the corridor towards the great oak door. The door creaked itself open again. He stood aside for them to walk in.

'I don't know if I can stand this,' thought Dad.

'What,' wondered Clara, 'if I suddenly get the hiccups?'

The Queen smiled and welcomed them to the Palace. She said she had been deeply worried about the state of the nation since the frightful viruses had started to appear. However, there did seem to be a way they might be stopped – and their dreadful perpetrator, too.

"It might be better for Quiddy to explain. Such a machine! I have never seen its like! Immune from viruses, too! And it is a vital part of our plan." She smiled down at Quiddy. "Will you continue?"

Quiddy smiled up at the Queen. Clara was struck with admiration, tinged with a smack of jealousy. It was almost as if Quiddy and the Queen were friends.

Then Quiddy, working away on the machine with her knee, told them about the Plan.

Chapter 11

A battle royal and a royal speech

The Queen and the gang walked back down the carpeted corridors, followed a few metres behind by Mr Stooping Stick Secretary. All the flunkies bowed as they went past. Patrick thought he'd make sure his device still worked. As they approached the last Palace flunkey he pressed it and asked cheerily, "Okay, mate?" The flunkey bowed low.

"Anything you wish is yours without question, Mr Pulgrove."

Two gleaming black limousines were waiting for them under the arches, with uniformed chauffeurs at the ready. Gold-braided guards opened the gleaming black doors. The Queen motioned to Quiddy to join her in the front car. Quiddy motioned to Dad to join her. Clara and the others moved towards the second car, but then Quiddy's machine called out, "Clara!" So Clara, with a wide grin, joined Quiddy and the Queen.

The chauffeur drove them smoothly, silently, out through the Palace gates and along the Mall. Here again, the people seemed mute and afraid. Clara was tempted to wave at them as though she had suddenly become a member of the Royal Family, but she didn't dare. Her heart was pounding, but it felt lighter than it had for days. Yes, she was jealous of Quiddy. But the two of them were friends, and as a gang they'd decided how to tackle

the mega-virus. Now the Queen was on their side.

Quiddy was thinking:

> *Wow! that bit worked! And something happened –
> or rather, the Queen and I have organised it so
> that something will happen – which the others
> would never, in a hundred thousand light years,
> guess could possibly happen!*

But, oddly, a quite different matter was on her mind as well. She wanted to ask Dad a question, privately. She typed on to her screen: "You forgot to say Mum's name. What is it?"

Dad looked at her, amazed. He mouthed, *"Now?"*

She nodded.

He lifted his shoulder in a gesture of helpless consent, leaned over and whispered in her ear.

"If you must know, it was Mavis."

Down Whitehall, past Horse Guards Parade and Downing Street. No doubt the Prime Minister was at this very moment in the House of Commons, uttering words of submission: "Anything you wish is yours without question, Sir Arthur." Then the limousine swept into Parliament Square and through the gates of the Houses of Parliament.

No need for a remote-control device to gain access here. One glance at the royal occupant of the front seat of the first limousine and they were through.

They stepped out of the limos amid more bowing flunkies, were ushered through more huge and impressive doors, propelled under echoing stone archways, persuaded through dark panelled corridors. Word had spread like wildfire through Parliament that "Ma'am" was here.

As they reached the last great doorway, Quiddy realised: not only were the gang to be on show to the whole of Parliament, they were on show to the whole country, maybe to the world. They walked through behind Her Majesty, feeling like ants approaching a herd of elephants. They gazed up and around them. High above them hung the television arc-lights; ranged round the room stood, like narrow-waisted robots, the television cameras.

The chamber was full. The atmosphere was tense. The Speaker sat on a stool beside her usual chair, anxiously knotting and unknotting the bow of her striped silk blouse. Balanced on the Speaker's chair, as he had been on television the previous day, stood Sir Arthur King. Beside the chair stood Patrick's dad.

Quiddy felt Clara's hand on her shoulder, comforting and warm. She glanced up, first at Clara, then at Patrick. Would he be able to play his part? Or would he be tempted to go back to the other side? He gave a nervous watery smile and nodded. Well, there was nothing else for it: she'd have to trust him.

Sir Arthur was taking no chances. He felt quickly in his left trouser pocket and brought out a small, black, rectangular object.

"Ah!" he called out harshly down the length of the chamber. "Your Majesty, I bid you welcome! And those little NIPpers, too – including my own flesh-and-blood, my nephew, Patrick Pulgrove! Honourable members of this House, witness now the humiliation of one who refused to obey his uncle's command!" He lifted the black rectangle and pressed.

All eyes were on Patrick. His shoulders drooped in the face of his illustrious relative. His voice came out in a cringing whine.

"Uncle Arthur, you are the big cheese, the gaffer, high monkey-monk, king fish, main man, top dog, blue-eyed boy, a straight shooter, curly wolf. You lay down the law, you crack the whip, you're in the driving seat, you have the clout, the final cut, the say-so in all our affairs. No need to pull the wool over our eyes or take us to the cleaners. We'll give you the green light, roll with the punches and swallow it whole."

Quiddy kicked him. Patrick looked surprised. Then his shoulders straightened and he remembered the Plan. He felt for his own infecting device and, his hand trembling, took it out and aimed it at his uncle.

Sir Arthur, too, looked surprised. The television cameras whirred and swung, their operators focusing on every detailed feature of his dark, powerful face. In homes hundreds of miles away children and parents, shopkeepers and factory workers, people in offices and boardrooms, waited breathlessly to hear what he had to say.

He turned pink, got down off the Speaker's chair, leaned forward and spoke with gaiety.

"Well, I should be so lucky!" He waved at Patrick over the assembled heads. "Fair enough, all the way. Is that good or is that good! You're a peach, young Patrick – you're singing my song! I'll bat, I'll go overboard, because I've got a real soft spot for you. Can I do anything for you – a write-up, a build-up or a thumbs up? That's the stuff to give to the troops, is what I say!" Then he looked again at the instrument in his hand. As if mystified he pointed it in Patrick's direction and pressed it again.

The MPs, puzzled and a little relieved not to be the subject of Sir Arthur's attentions at the moment, looked from uncle to nephew and back again as if they were watching the tennis at Wimbledon.

Patrick's face was pink, too, as he answered.

"Don't you think we should hang up our tools, Uncle Arthur – pack it in and call it a day? After all, the country doesn't want to footle about, scrimshank or skive off. People want to get stuck in, they want to zing, to zip, they want to buzz around like a one-armed paperhanger. They don't want to have their arms twisted or feel the screws on. They need to be footloose and fancy-free, to feel the sky's the limit."

Quiddy was confused. Was this one of Uncle Arthur's viruses, or was Patrick playing around for his own amusement? She kicked him again. He grinned at her and zapped his instrument once more.

Sir Arthur was trying to distract attention from Patrick and, in as dictatorial a voice as he could muster, was beginning a speech, "The first duty of every citizen is to obey the dictates of his superior. His superior, in all cases and at all times, is of course …"

Then he caught Patrick's zap, and instantly changed his tune. "Yes, my boy, you're absolutely right. I've come a cropper, gone off the rails and fouled it up. I'm a waste of space, a dead duck, a wash-out, a write-off. I don't amount to a pot full of crabapples. But, when the chips are down, I hope you'll let me do a runner and head for the hills. When all's said and done, we've got to stick our necks out and save our own bacon."

Clara nudged Quiddy. Her head was splitting.

"Please," she whispered. "I can't stand any more! Stop them!"

Quiddy was quite enjoying the spectacle but she knew Clara was right. It was time. She howled.

It was then that Her Majesty the Queen stepped forward – according to the Plan. The House hushed at her movement. Even Sir Arthur, beetroot red and still mystified, held his peace.

But the Queen did not speak. She took a couple more steps till she was very close to Quiddy. Then she leaned over the machine and pressed a key. Quiddy's voice rang round the chamber – but they were the Queen's words.

"Sir Arthur King – or rather, the so-called Sir Arthur King, for we have not conferred a knighthood on such a man – step forward."

The gang – Clara, Amelia, Geoffrey and the twins – held their breath and reached for each other's hands.

They knew why the Queen dared not speak: Sir Arthur King's mega-virus might affect her, as it had done on that first Leonardo-infected day during the State Opening of Parliament. But Quiddy's machine was immune. The Queen had programmed in her speech. Now it emerged: the royal words in Quiddy's electronic mid-Atlantic voice.

Arthur King, as if propelled by a robot, stood forward. His accomplice, Patrick's father, also stood forward.

"An attempt has been made to usurp the democratic powers of this ancient House of Commons and to overturn the personal autonomy of the individual citizens of our land."

Quiddy, in her chair beside the Queen, listened. She already knew what the Queen was going to say, but it was different now. The world was paying attention.

"No Head of State can countenance such seizure of power by whatever method, be it by infiltration or subjugation or, as in the present circumstances, by subtle interference with the means of recognised current communication."

The twins were whispering.

"What's she on about?" "Haven't the foggiest!"

Clara hissed at them, "Ssshhh!"

"We are no exception. This House is supreme in the land and we as monarch uphold it. It is our duty, therefore, to seize the weapons of destruction and confiscate them. Owners of these weapons, come here!"

There was a moment of complete and utter quiet. Even the television cameras seemed to stop whirring. The chamber – full to bursting with MPs, media people, the Queen's retinue and the gang – was hushed and still.

Quiddy waited for Patrick. She knew he would have to move first. But she knew, too, that the use of power had made him feel extraordinary, sensational, high. It was a drug.

Would he budge? Would he give it up?

He didn't.

But Sir Arthur King, followed like a twin by Patrick's faithful father, came down from his place at the Speaker's chair. Still mystified by all the happenings of the last half-hour, the colour draining from his face, he walked slowly down the aisle of the House to where the Queen and the gang were gathered.

He's a man of power. He wants people to knuckle under to him – but when he's beaten he'll throw in the towel faster than a rat runs up a drain, quick as greased lightning, before you can say Jack Robinson. Whoops! Haven't caught it myself, have I?

Her Majesty held out a hand towards Patrick, a hand towards Sir Arthur. Sir Arthur stretched forward and laid the small, destructive implement on the royal palm. She looked expectantly at Patrick.

"Now, Patrick," thought Quiddy. "Don't let us down."

Patrick's blue eyes twinkled.

"Certainly, Ma'am. In a moment. Would you mind? Just an experiment – a joke ..."

He walked past his uncle and his father – "Excuse me, Dad" – to the despatch box where the Prime Minister sat. Clara whispered to Quiddy.

"Have you heard Patrick's dad say a single word, ever?"

Patrick stood in front of the Prime Minister and aimed his device. He looked round, grinned at the television cameras and said, "My mum says that Prime Ministers never say this – and they often should."

Then he pressed. The Prime Minister, turning pink, pronounced the unprecedented words, "I'm sorry, I was wrong."

The whole House erupted in laughter and tears and fury and elation. Patrick walked back and gave his device to the Queen.

"Hurray!" shouted the children. They waved at every television camera in sight. "Three cheers!"

"Hello Mum – are you watching?" called Amelia.

"Mum – I'm fine! How are you?" shouted Geoffrey.

Above the clamour, the Queen's voice could just be heard:

"We do feel that congratulations are due to these young people here. Shall we have a round of applause for them – especially for Quiddy?"

"Quiddy's the greatest," came the chorus. "Hurray!"

Chapter 12

An end and a beginning

The police were waiting for Uncle Arthur. He stood, alone and forlorn, while a tide of blue uniforms surrounded him. As the handcuffs clicked, Clara whispered to Quiddy, "What will they charge him with? Forcing the wrong words out of people isn't a crime, is it?"

They listened and heard the police chief say: "Breach of the peace – affray – attempt to pervert the course of justice – treason."

Where was Patrick's father? It seemed he had progressed from being silent to being invisible. He had completely disappeared.

But what about Patrick himself? He's committed some of the same crimes. Where's he got to? Has he done a disappearing act too? No, he's over there, hiding between the twins. He's probably hoping to look like a triplet – but he's miles taller than Matt and Mike! Will the police arrest him and take him away?

A trickle of blue uniforms were separating themselves from the rest. They moved purposefully in the direction of Matt, Mike and Patrick.

But the Queen moved purposefully in that direction too. The blue uniforms stood to attention as if struck with a virus.

"Your Majesty!"

"Gentlemen," she said. "Do not arrest this boy. My young informants here tell me that he acted solely under the influence of his uncle. He has been instrumental in bringing the crisis to a successful conclusion."

Patrick gave a whoop of relief.

"That means it wasn't my fault and I helped to sort things out so I'm going to be all right!" he told the twins gleefully.

The Queen led the way out of the House, with Quiddy whizzing along beside her, trying with some difficulty not to overtake. The gang followed, with Quiddy's dad following close behind.

All over the country, doorbells were ringing and phones were buzzing with the sound of families and friends and neighbours and factories and businesses and shops all communicating freely with each other again.

Back in Quiddy's house, the telephone rang. But there was no one to answer it.

"A gala reception at the Palace?" Dad looked as if he'd been invited to a thieves' breakfast at Brixton Jail.

Quiddy felt sorry for him. The day had been more of a strain on him than on any of them, because he'd had nothing to do except worry about things going wrong. She consulted with the gang, then with Her Majesty, and came back to him.

"Cuppa tea?" she asked. "In not-so-posh part of Palace?"

Dad nodded glumly.

"If I've got to."

"You've got to!" shouted the others. The Queen smiled.

As they sped in the limousines back through the gates of Buckingham Palace, the crowds cheered and the cameras whirred again.

"I wonder if my mum's watching," murmured Amelia to Geoffrey in the back of the second limo.

"I bet mine is," he replied.

Silver salvers laden with crust-free salmon sandwiches ... champagne glasses filled to overflowing with pure orange and pineapple juice ... cakes with thick white creamy cream oozing out of every crevice ...

"If this is afternoon tea," muttered Patrick, "what on earth's a state banquet?"

"Come on, Quid," begged Dad, after an hour. He was balancing a delicate china cup on the palm of one beefy hand while holding a crisp, linen napkin between the fingers of that hand and clutching a plate full of crumbs in the other. "Let's go home."

Quiddy was worn out. She knew they'd got a long journey ahead of them. She programmed in a message to the gang and whizzed round them showing it to each one on her screen.

"Time to go, folks."

They said their thank-yous to the Queen and Mr Stick Secretary. Her Majesty knelt down on the carpet to say goodbye to Quiddy, so as to be down at her level. The Queen, kneeling to Quiddy! Clara had to stifle a laugh. She wasn't jealous any more. Like the others, she was just longing to get home.

The flunkeys bowed to them as they walked out, without any need for Patrick's virus-infecting device. A single, long limo with three rows of passenger seats drove them through London to the station. Cheerful people on the pavements stopped their chattering for a moment to see if there was anyone royal inside.

"They don't know it's us," said Patrick proudly. "But we're the ones who saved the country!"

He seems to have forgotten that he helped to start the trouble in the first place. Oh well, we won't remind him.

The gang all fell asleep in the train. Mostly they dreamed about red carpets and cream cakes. Quiddy dreamed about telephones ringing in an empty house. Only Dad stayed awake, struggling with the last of his crossword clues and wondering what he'd done to deserve a day – and a daughter – like this.

Geoffrey spent the last of his money on a taxi that would go round all their houses and drop each one of them off at home.

When the twins arrived back, their parents said, "Oh, is it you? We saw you on the telly. Off you go to bed."

But Mike and Matt weren't having it. They jumped up and down and thumped the table and stamped their feet until they had the entire family's full attention.

"Right!" they announced. "You're going to listen to us, for once. Just hear this!"

They held their family riveted for two whole hours

without a break.

Amelia's mother was waiting at the door. She looked as though she'd been standing there all day without even going inside to make a cup of tea.

She rushed to Amelia and enfolded her in her arms. "Amelia, my poppet, my pet! I saw you waving – I saw you with the Queen! You looked so neat – and you behaved so well! I'm so proud of you ... But what's that blob on your skirt? Amelia! It's strawberry jam!"

Amelia giggled. "Don't fuss, Mum," she breathed. "It is *Buckingham Palace* strawberry jam."

Geoffrey's mum, too, was waiting at the door. She'd heard the taxi and knew it must be her boy.

"Geoffrey, love! You called to me through the television!" She ran down the path from the bungalow. "Are you hungry after your hectic day? Are you sure you've been eating properly?"

"You bet, Mum! You should have seen the cream cakes at Buck House!"

"Cream cakes? Dear dear – so full of cholesterol! I do hope it was *fresh* cream. Oh, Geoffrey, is all this going to give you another upset tummy?"

"Hush, Mum," he said to her gently. "It's not going to upset anyone. And I don't want anything to eat. All I want now is a mug of cocoa, while you listen to me telling you all about our day."

Patrick's mum had been alerted by Geoffrey's and Amelia's and was walking along the road to meet them. The taxi pulled up. Quiddy and Clara watched as Patrick and his mother walked hand in hand along the street towards home.

Then it was Clara's turn. When they reached the house, Quiddy pressed the key to say the short sentence that she'd programmed in – so long before it seemed like centuries ago.

It said:

YOU ARE MY FRIEND.

Clara gave her a hug.

"You're my friend too." She got out and went to her front door.

The taxi drew up outside Quiddy's house.

"Right, love," said Dad. "Out we get." The taxi-driver opened the boot and Dad lifted out the wheelchair.

Quiddy sat in the taxi waiting for Dad to pick her up. She glanced at the house. There was a figure at the door. It would be one of the neighbours waiting to hear a blow-by-blow account of the happenings in London, no doubt.

Dad carried her out of the taxi, put her down in her chair and strapped her in as usual. She let him go through the garden gate in front of her because he'd got the key to the house. Halfway down the path she nearly bumped into him. He'd stopped in his tracks.

She pressed a key. "What's going on?"

He stepped out of her way so that she could see the person at the front door more clearly. He said something – just one word – but she couldn't hear it properly because he sort of gasped it.

The person was a woman – and it wasn't a neighbour.

Quiddy didn't recognise her. She had hair about the same colour as Quiddy's. She looked very nervous.

Quiddy stopped whizzing. She didn't know what to do. She couldn't go into the house because the woman was standing between her and the door. In any case, Dad had got to unlock the door, and Dad seemed to have gone back somewhere near the garden gate.

The woman said, "Quiddy!"

Quiddy heard Dad's voice behind her. He said the same word as he'd said before, but this time she could hear it. "Mavis!"

But in the instant before he said it, she knew who the woman was. She did recognise her – not with the memory in her brain, but with a different kind of memory: one of warmth, closeness and softness, followed by loss, sadness and grief.

The woman said, with a voice that sounded choked, "I saw you, Quiddy. I saw you in Parliament with the Queen. I saw what you could do and what you could say."

She paused. Quiddy knew she couldn't find the words for how she felt.

Then she found some words.

"Oh, Quiddy, I feel like the Prime Minister!"

Quiddy was crying. She couldn't think what her mother meant. Like the Prime Minister? What did the Prime Minister feel like?

Her mum said, "I left you because I thought you weren't any good. I'd wanted you to be like your twin. Then she died and I was upset. I thought you'd be a

burden. But ... No one's forcing me to say it, Quiddy. This is what I really mean. I'm sorry, I was wrong."

Now Quiddy was laughing as well as crying. Dad hadn't any idea what to say or do, so he got out his key, opened the front door and let them in. Then he put on the kettle for a strong cup of tea.

Hours later, as Dad was about to carry her upstairs to bed, Quiddy said, "Mum?"

"Yes, love?"

She'd got ready what she wanted to say. "Why did you call me such a peculiar name? I like it, but it is very strange."

"I didn't know what to call you," said her mum. "I wanted you to have an interesting name. Not like mine. I mean – Mavis!" Quiddy couldn't see what was wrong with Mavis, but she didn't interrupt. "I looked through the book of names a hundred times," her mum went on, "and I couldn't find a thing I liked. Then I got the dictionary. I thought, something in this dictionary must give me some sort of idea.' I went through it from A onwards. It took me hours. I'd got as far as Q before I found it. The word I picked was 'quiddity'. I thought, Quiddy! That's it!"

Quiddy looked at her, head on one side. She wanted to ask, "But what does that mean?"

Her mum understood.

"It means, 'I am what I am'," she said. "I said to your dad, 'I'll call her Quiddy, after that word'. So we did. And you are what you are. And it's okay."